P9-DIW-470

Once Upon a Time...

Cover illustrated by Jon Goodell
Title page illustrated by Yoshiko Jaeggi

Phoenix International Publications, Inc.
8501 West Higgins Road, Suite 300, Chicago, Illinois 60631
Lower Ground Floor, 59 Gloucester Place, London W1U 8JJ

www.pikidsmedia.com

8 7 6 5 4 3 2 1

ISBN: 978-1-4127-6332-5

Once Upon a Time

A TREASURY OF FAIRY TALES

pi kids®
phoenix international publications, inc.

TABLE of CONTENTS

Cinderella

Adapted by Caleb Burroughs
Illustrated by Yoshiko Jaeggi

Many, many years ago, there lived a beautiful girl who was cursed with a very mean, very ugly stepmother. Not only was the girl's stepmother mean and ugly, but the woman also had two daughters who were even meaner and uglier than she.

Now, this dreadful stepmother expected her kind and beautiful stepdaughter to do all of the dirtiest household chores. The girl peeled the potatoes and scrubbed the floors. She washed the dishes and split the firewood.

But none of these tasks was as dirty as scooping the cinders and ash from the fireplace.

"Cinderella!" her stepsisters would chant. "Clean the cinders, Cinderella!"

"Cinderella," her stepmother would demand, "clean the fireplace until it shines! I don't want to see a single cinder left!"

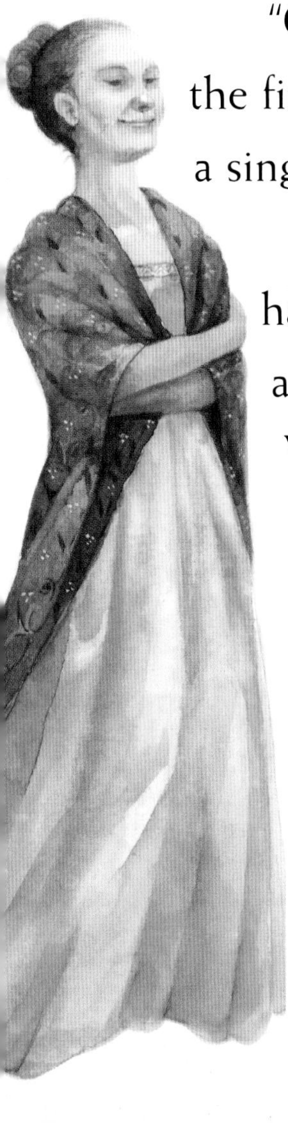

So the beautiful girl worked hard, covered in dirt and ash, and the awful name clung to her. While her stepsisters wore gorgeous gowns and jewelry and flowers in their hair, the girl now known as Cinderella wore rags and scrubbed the filthy fireplace.

One day, a messenger arrived with a very important delivery. It was an invitation to the prince's royal ball.

"Oooh!" squealed one of the terrible stepsisters. "I hope the handsome prince will ask me to dance with him!"

"He will surely ask me," said the other stepsister. "I am the most beautiful young lady in all the kingdom!"

"I know the prince will be enchanted by both of you," declared their mother. "You are both lucky to be blessed with my good looks—unlike our little Cinderella."

The three women then turned to look at poor Cinderella. They teased her for being dirty and for wearing rags.

Soon, the night of the ball arrived. The stepsisters excitedly squeezed into their finest gowns. They made Cinderella help them fasten their necklaces and style their hair. All the while, they scolded her and taunted her because she would not be going to the ball.

"Ouch! You are pulling my hair!" yelled one stepsister.

"While we are dancing with the handsome prince, Cinderella will be tidying the house," laughed the other.

Cinderella watched sadly as they left for the ball.

When she was alone, Cinderella sat down in the garden and sobbed.

"Why must I work all day long and be so wretched and dirty?" poor Cinderella asked herself. "If only I could go and dance at the ball, just for one night!" No sooner had she spoken these words than Cinderella was surprised by a flash of light. Before her appeared a winged woman dressed in a flowing gown.

"Who are you?" asked a very startled Cinderella.

"Why, I'm your fairy godmother," answered the woman.

"My fairy godmother?" asked Cinderella.

"Yes, my dear," said the woman. "I am here to help you. I have watched while your family has mistreated you, and I have come to help bring you the good fortune you deserve. Tonight is the night of the royal ball, is it not? Would you like to go?"

"More than anything!" answered Cinderella. "My stepsisters have already gone. But I must stay here. I have nothing to wear but these filthy rags."

"Leave that to me," said the fairy godmother.

With a wave of her wand, the fairy godmother showered the garden with sparks. When Cinderella opened her eyes she was amazed by what she saw.

"Why, my rags have turned into a beautiful gown!" exclaimed Cinderella. "Look at these lovely glass slippers! The pumpkins and mice from the garden are a coach and a team of fine horses! How did you do this?"

"There is no time for questions, my dear," said the fairy godmother. "You must hurry to the ball, for my magic spell will be broken once the clock strikes twelve."

Dressed in her splendid gown and riding in her fine horse-drawn coach, Cinderella arrived at the ball.

"Who is that stunning girl?" asked one of the guests.

"She must be royalty," said another.

Seeing the gorgeous young woman, the prince asked her to dance. With a warm smile, Cinderella agreed.

"Who does that girl think she is?" cried the two stepsisters, not knowing the stranger was really Cinderella.

Throughout the night, the prince danced only with Cinderella. The other girls had come to the ball hoping to dance with him, and perhaps make him fall in love with them. But the prince's eyes never left Cinderella—and she never left his arms.

"I have never had such a wonderful time," Cinderella told the prince. Dancing with him, she felt herself falling in love.

The prince was falling in love, too.

"Who are you?" he asked Cinderella.

Before Cinderella could answer, the clock began to strike twelve. She had forgotten all about her fairy godmother's warning!

As the clock chimed, Cinderella rushed from the prince's arms.

"I must get home," she thought to herself. "I cannot let the prince see me in my filthy rags."

"Come back!" cried the startled prince. "You did not even tell me your name!"

But Cinderella did not hear him, for she was already out of the palace doors. She flew down the steps. In her hurry, she had dropped one of her glass slippers.

The prince rushed after her. He did not see the beautiful girl that he loved, but he did find one of her glass slippers.

Picking it up, he vowed he would see her again.

The next day, Cinderella was again in her rags, cleaning her stepmother's house.

As she scrubbed, she heard her stepsisters talking excitedly. "The prince is searching the kingdom for the girl he loves," said one.

"He has her glass slipper with him. Whomever it fits, he will marry," said the other stepsister.

Soon, the prince arrived at the house of Cinderella's stepmother.

Cinderella watched, hidden in a corner, as each of her selfish stepsisters tried on the slipper. But their feet were far too big for the delicate shoe. The prince was standing to leave when he spotted Cinderella.

"Won't you try on the slipper?" asked the prince.

"Dirty Cinderella?" laughed the wicked stepmother. "Certainly she is not the girl you love!"

But the prince insisted. Sure enough, Cinderella's dainty foot fit perfectly inside the glass slipper. The prince had found his love at last!

Cinderella and the prince were soon married. They lived happily ever after.

Rapunzel

Adapted by Caleb Burroughs
Illustrated by Kathi Ember

There once was a powerful and dreadful witch. This witch lived in a high castle that overlooked a garden. And in this garden grew the freshest and most beautiful fruits and vegetables.

Next to the witch's land stood a sad and tiny ramshackle cottage in which lived a poor man and his wife. The wife was expecting the couple's first child.

One evening, the couple sat eating their dinner of hard bread and cold beans when the wife had a craving.

"My dear husband," she said, "I would love just a nibble of the fresh rapunzel lettuce that grows in the witch's garden. It would taste so much better than these cold beans and stale bread."

So later that night, the poor man climbed the fence to the witch's garden and headed into the patch of rapunzel lettuce.

Just as he knelt to pick the freshest head of lettuce he could find, the man heard a wicked cackle. He spun around to see the witch!

"How dare you enter my garden!" screeched the witch. "And what do I see? You were trying to steal some of my delicious rapunzel lettuce? Why, I never!"

The man cowered among the vegetables, begging the angry witch not to hurt him. "I meant no harm. I was merely trying to pick a bit for my hungry wife," he cried. "Let me go home to her, for she is expecting our first child."

"Go home," replied the witch. "Take all that you want from my garden. But when your child comes, I shall take her for my own!"

The scared man climbed back over the garden wall and hurried home, his pockets full of rapunzel lettuce.

His wife ate her fill of the fresh lettuce. She loved it so much that she decided to name her child after the delicious vegetable. Her husband did not tell her about the witch's nasty threat.

A short time later, a baby girl was born. The woman named her child Rapunzel. Later that day, there was a knock on the door. It was the witch!

"As I promised," said the witch, "I am here to take your child."

"What is she talking about?" the woman asked her husband. But the poor couple could do nothing, and the witch took the child from them.

Now, while this witch was very mean, she was also very smart. She knew that the child's parents might try to find her, so she locked little Rapunzel in a high tower.

Days turned into months, and months turned into years, while little Rapunzel grew from an infant into a beautiful young woman.

During her many years in the tower, Rapunzel had never been allowed to cut her hair. So it had grown long—very, very long.

Her two golden braids had grown so long, in fact, that the witch put them to good use. The window to Rapunzel's tower room was very high, so to reach it, the witch would call:

"Rapunzel, Rapunzel,
Throw down your gold hair!"

Rapunzel would obey, and the witch would scurry up the two golden braids.

One day, a handsome prince was traveling through the forest. From a distance, he heard a girl's voice singing a lovely song. He was following the sound of the beautiful voice when suddenly he heard a scratchy, ugly voice croak:

"Rapunzel, Rapunzel,

Throw down your gold hair!"

Through his spyglass, the prince was surprised to see a beautiful girl with long golden hair. She was perched in a tower window. He spotted an ugly old witch climbing up her golden braids.

In his hiding spot in the woods, the handsome prince waited until the old witch left the tower. Enchanted by the beautiful girl and her lovely voice, the curious prince crept up to the tower and called:

"Rapunzel, Rapunzel,
Throw down your gold hair!"

Sure enough, as soon as the prince had finished saying these words, two golden braids of hair fell from the high window. Taking hold of them, the prince climbed up the tower wall, where he reached the beautiful girl.

"Who are you?" the prince asked.

"I am Rapunzel," she replied. "An old witch took me from my parents when I was but a baby. I have lived locked in this tower ever since."

"I will save you," said the prince.

He climbed down the tower wall to the ground below. There he stood while Rapunzel leaped from the window into his arms.

No sooner had the prince rescued the beautiful young girl than the witch returned to the tower. Quickly, the prince and Rapunzel hid in the bushes. From their hiding place, they heard the witch call:

"Rapunzel, Rapunzel,

Throw down your gold hair!"

This time, no braids of golden hair fell from the high window. This was a shock to the old witch, who yelled, "Alas, Rapunzel has escaped from my tower! Now I will be all alone for the rest of my days!"

Rapunzel and the prince stayed hidden and watched as the old witch wandered off into the forest, whining and moaning and gnashing her teeth at having lost the prisoner from her tower.

Once they could no longer hear the witch, the prince helped Rapunzel onto his horse and away they rode.

After riding for some time, the prince and Rapunzel finally arrived at the home of her parents. It had been many years since the witch had stolen their child, and the poor man and his wife had grown very old.

Yet their sad faces disappeared when they saw the beautiful girl with the golden hair.

"I am your daughter, Rapunzel," said the girl. "This brave and handsome prince rescued me from the old witch. He would like for all of us to come live in his castle."

And that is exactly what they did, living happily ever after.

Puss in Boots

Adapted by Harry Kryst
Illustrated by Victoria and Julius Lisi

Like so many stories, this one begins once upon a time. This tale will reveal how a very unlikely person managed to marry the daughter of a king.

The story begins with a cat called Puss, who belonged to an old farmer. After living a long and happy life, the old farmer passed away, leaving his farm to his sons. The youngest son was the most saddened by the loss of his father. It was for this reason Puss decided to make this son his new master. Puss felt certain that he could help the young man.

As it happened, Puss had a wonderful speaking voice. "I'm at your service," Puss said to the youngest son.

"I'm afraid not," said the young man. "I cannot afford to take care of you."

"Ah, my master," replied Puss, "but it is I who will take care of you. I ask for only two things: a pair of boots and a sack."

The son hesitated, trying to figure out why a cat would want boots and a sack. Seeing no harm in it, he agreed.

"I have an old pair of boots you may use," said the son. "And a sack."

Puss bowed before the young farmer and promised to do his best to make life better for him.

Puss set off into the forest. With his boots, Puss was able to hike deep into the woods, where the fattest rabbits lived. Puss had a plan to trap a rabbit. It would make the perfect meal for his new master.

It didn't take long for a skilled hunter like Puss to succeed in his mission. In no time, his sack was heavy with one of the biggest rabbits the forest had to offer. This rabbit was so magnificent, in fact, that it was fit for a king—which gave Puss an idea.

Rather than taking his prize home to his master, Puss went straight to the king's palace. He informed a guard that he had a gift for the king. When the guard saw the beautiful rabbit, he bowed and allowed the mysterious visitor access to the king straightaway.

"This may be the finest rabbit I have ever laid eyes on," bellowed the king. "From whom do you bear this gift?"

Puss bowed before the king and said, "It is a gift from my master. He is the Duke of Carabas."

"I have not heard of this duke," said the king. "But such a magnificent gift will not be forgotten."

Puss bowed once again and took leave of the king. He returned to the castle every day for a week, each time bringing another gift to the king.

Puss had planted a very important seed in the mind of the king. He made the king think that Puss's master was a great and wealthy duke. One day, Puss learned that the king's carriage would be passing by his master's farm. The clever Puss devised a plan to help his master.

"Master, forgive me for what I am about to do," said Puss. And he shoved his master right into the river that flowed along the road.

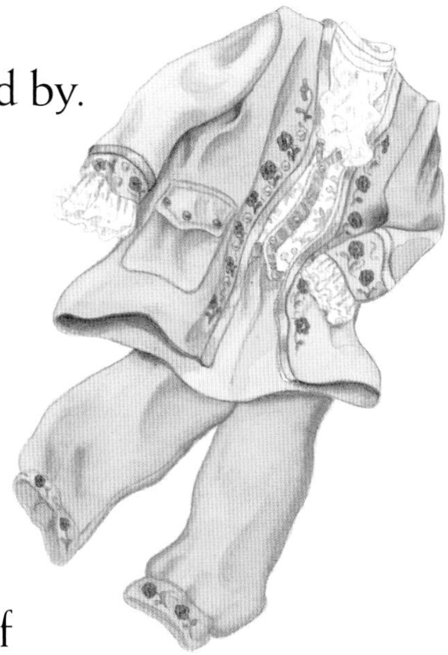

"Help! Help!" yelled Puss as the king passed by. "My master is drowning. The Duke of Carabas has been robbed!"

The king ordered his men to stop at once. They ran to the riverbed and pulled the young farmer from the water.

"My goodness," said the king to the young man. "I am delighted to finally meet the Duke of Carabas. Your gifts these past weeks have been very generous. I hope that now I may return the favor."

The king ordered his men to fetch a set of the king's finest clothes. In no time, the young farmer was dry and sitting next to the king and the king's daughter in their private carriage.

Puss smiled to himself as his plan continued to work. "Now for the next step," said Puss.

The king offered the Duke of Carabas a ride home. Puss ran ahead of the carriage. He spotted some farmhands working on the land along the road. Puss quickly explained to the workers that when the king passed by, they were to say that they were working on land that belonged to the Duke of Carabas.

Sure enough, no sooner had the carriage arrived than the king leaned out to ask the workers, "Tell me, for whom do you labor?"

"We work for the Duke of Carabas. He owns all of this land," the farmers said.

The king turned to his guest and said, "You are a wealthy duke, indeed. I would enjoy seeing your home."

Puss quickly realized that something had to be done. His master's home was certainly not fit for a duke. So once again, Puss ran ahead of the carriage. He soon came to a great castle in which dwelled a fearsome giant.

This was no ordinary giant—it was a giant who possessed magical powers. Puss knew he faced a challenge, but being the clever cat he was, he came up with a plan in no time.

Puss sneaked into the giant's castle and found the giant cooking a great feast in his kitchen.

"What are you doing in my castle?" roared the giant.

"It is said that you're a very powerful giant," said Puss.

"That is true," said the giant. "I'm more powerful than the king. For I can change myself into a fierce lion, a huge mountain, a deadly viper, or even a thunderous cloud."

"Ah," said Puss. "But are you so powerful that you could turn yourself into something very tiny? Say, a mouse?"

"Ha," laughed the giant, "how dare you question my power. I will show you." With that, the giant spun around until he was just a tiny mouse.

Wasting no time, Puss leaped on the mouse and, like cats will do, ate the mouse right up. The giant's castle now belonged to Puss and his master. And not a moment too soon, for the king's carriage was arriving.

Puss ran to meet the carriage. "Welcome to the duke's humble castle," he said. "We have a feast awaiting us."

The king—and his daughter—were impressed by the wealthy duke. And the duke was charmed by the lovely princess. This was how they fell in love and how an unlikely man married a princess.

Puss in Boots lived the rest of his days in royal comfort.

Little Red Riding Hood

Adapted by Lawrence A. West
Illustrated by Thea Kliros

In a small town, next to a large forest, there lived a little girl. She was called Little Red Riding Hood because of the cape her grandmother had made for her.

One day her mother said, "Grandmother is sick. Please take her this basket of goodies. Be sure that you stay on the path."

"All right, Mother," said Little Red Riding Hood, and she set off with the basket.

Little Red Riding Hood soon forgot her mother's warning. She wandered off the path and into the fragrant woods. There she met a wolf. She did not know anything about hungry wolves, and so she was not afraid.

"Where are you going, little girl?" asked the wolf. "What do you have in that basket?"

"I am going to visit my grandmother, who lives in the house with the red door," answered the girl. "She is sick, and I am taking her a basket of treats."

"Do you have any fresh strawberries in your basket?" asked the wolf.

"No," admitted Red Riding Hood.

"Surely your grandmother would like some," said the wolf. "My grandmother loves strawberries."

Little Red Riding Hood thought for a moment. Then she decided that the wolf was right. "I will run and pick some right now," she said.

"You can leave your basket with me," suggested the hungry wolf. "I would be happy to watch it for you while you are gone."

"No, thank you," said Red Riding Hood. "I will bring it with me, so I can carry the strawberries."

The disappointed wolf watched Little Red Riding Hood hurry away. He was very hungry, and a basket of goodies sounded delicious.

Just as he was about to give up, Little Red Riding Hood came skipping back toward him. It was then that he came up with a plan.

"I see that you do not have any flowers for your grandmother," said the wolf. "I have just picked this bouquet for my own grandmother. I suggest you pick one, too. I know your grandmother would like it."

"Grandmother does love flowers," said Little Red Riding Hood. And she began to search for the loveliest yellow and white blooms she could find. So busy was she that she did not see the wolf run off in the direction of Grandmother's little house.

Little Red Riding Hood gathered her bouquet of flowers and skipped off to deliver her gifts. At the same time, the wolf snuck into Grandmother's house. He frightened her so greatly that she ran out of the front door!

Then the wolf dressed in one of Grandmother's nightgowns. He put on a sleeping bonnet and slipped into Grandmother's comfortable bed to wait for Little Red Riding Hood.

The wolf did not have to wait long. In a moment he heard the front door open.

"Hello, Grandmother," called Little Red Riding Hood.

"Hello, dear," said the wolf in a disguised voice. "Please come in. I am resting in bed."

Red Riding Hood walked into Grandmother's room.

"I hope you are feeling better, Grandmother," she said. "I brought you a basket of goodies from Mother and me."

"Thank you, my dear," said the wolf. "That is most kind. I am feeling better now. Your basket of goodies certainly smells delicious. Please, come closer, and give me some news from the village."

Little Red Riding Hood stepped closer to the bed. Her grandmother looked very strange! The girl was surprised to see that her grandmother's eyes looked much larger than she remembered.

"Why, Grandmother," said Little Red Riding Hood, "what big eyes you have!"

The wolf blinked, trying to hide them from her.

"All the better to see you with, my dear," he said.

As the wolf shifted in the bed to hide his eyes, the bonnet slipped from his head.

"Why, Grandmother," said Little Red Riding Hood, "what big ears you have!"

"All the better to hear you with, my dear," said the wolf.

As the wolf reached up to fix the bonnet on his head, he let the covers slip from his face.

"Why, Grandmother," said Little Red Riding Hood, "what big teeth you have!"

"All the better to EAT you with!" cried the wolf.

With that, Little Red Riding Hood let out a scream and ran from the room. The wolf leaped from the bed and chased after her.

When the wolf reached out to grab her cape, she knocked over a chair and ran away.

"Stop!" cried a loud voice, suddenly.

Little Red Riding Hood looked back to see a woodcutter holding his ax in the air.

"Do you think you scare me?" asked the wolf.

"I believe I should," said the woodcutter. He reached for the wolf and grabbed him by the tail. Then the woodcutter carried the wolf into the forest.

As he did so, Grandmother came running up to Little Red Riding Hood. She had been hiding nearby, in the garden shed.

"Grandmother, I am so glad you are safe!" cried Red Riding Hood. "I was worried that the wolf had eaten you."

Grandmother gave Little Red Riding Hood a great big hug as the woodcutter came out of the woods.

"I do not think that wolf will trouble you again," he said, adjusting his cap.

"Thank you very much," said Grandmother. "Won't you please join us for a snack?"

The woodcutter, Little Red Riding Hood, and Grandmother enjoyed the basket of goodies as they sat and told stories for the rest of the day.

Now whenever Red Riding Hood visits her grandmother, she is careful to stay on the path.

Jack and the Beanstalk

Adapted by Jane Jerrard
Illustrated by Sue Williams

There was once a poor widow who lived with her son Jack. They made a meager living selling milk. When one day their cow Milky-white gave no milk, his mother told Jack to take the cow to market and sell her for a good price. They were very sorry to lose her, but they needed the money for food.

On his way to market, Jack met a strange man who asked him where he was taking the cow.

"I am going to market to sell her," he said.

"You look like a sharp young man," said the stranger. "I will give you these five magic beans for your cow."

Jack was delighted with the offer. He swiftly made the trade and hurried home.

"Look what I got in exchange for the cow!" he said eagerly.

"You foolish boy!" cried Jack's mother, tossing the beans out the window. "Now we must go to bed hungry."

When Jack awoke early the next morning, he noticed an odd shadow falling across his window. He ran outside and saw that a huge beanstalk had sprung up during the night! It was so tall that the top disappeared into the clouds.

Jack was a very curious boy, and he decided to climb the beanstalk. He climbed and climbed for what seemed like hours, until he finally reached the top.

Jack could not believe what he saw! In front of him stood an enormous, magnificent castle.

Since his arms and legs felt so tired and sore, Jack knew that the long climb up the beanstalk had not been a mere dream. He rubbed his eyes to make sure he was not seeing things, but the castle still stood before him.

Curious as ever, Jack decided to walk to the castle. On the way there, he met a beautiful fairy. She told Jack about the greedy giant who lived in the castle. Long ago, she said, the terrible giant had stolen all of Jack's father's gold.

The fairy told Jack that the gold was rightfully his, and that he should take it back from the giant.

When Jack reached the steps of the castle, he was amazed at the size of everything.

Jack made his way to the kitchen, where he saw the giant asleep at a table. The giant had been counting gold coins when he nodded off.

Jack climbed onto the table and grabbed a bag of gold. But when he climbed down, he dropped the bag and woke the giant.

The giant sniffed the air and roared, "Fee-fi-fo-fum! I smell the blood of an Englishman!"

Jack was quite frightened. He grabbed the bag of gold and raced out of the castle as fast as his little feet would carry him.

The giant gave chase all the way back to the beanstalk, but Jack was faster. He threw the bag down to his mother's garden and scrambled down as quickly as he could. Jack's mother was overcome with joy when the gold coins rained down. She knew that she and Jack would never again go to bed hungry.

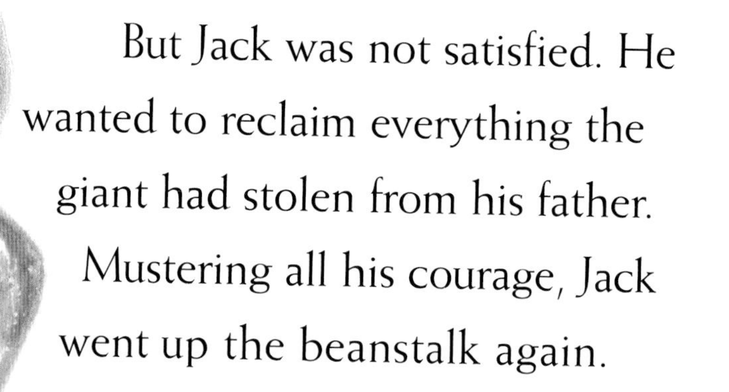

But Jack was not satisfied. He wanted to reclaim everything the giant had stolen from his father. Mustering all his courage, Jack went up the beanstalk again.

This time, when Jack returned to the castle, he ran into the giant's wife. He begged for her mercy. She was wary of helping Jack, but the little boy was so polite she could not resist.

She hid Jack in the oven when the giant stomped in for his supper.

"Fee-fi-fo-fum, I smell the blood of an Englishman!" roared the giant.

"Don't be silly, love," said the giant's wife. "It is only your supper."

The giant ate his meal and then he told his wife to bring him his hen.

Jack peeked out of the oven as he heard the giant shout, "Lay!"

On command, the hen laid a golden egg! The giant had the hen lay eggs until he finally fell asleep.

Jack leaped from the oven, snatched the hen, and hurried back down the beanstalk.

After quite some time had passed, Jack decided to climb the beanstalk again. Jack sneaked back into the castle, and this time he hid in a large pot.

The giant sniffed the air and searched the kitchen.

"Fee-fi-fo-fum! I smell the blood of an Englishman!" he roared. The giant was about to look into the pot where Jack was hiding, when his wife called him to supper.

After eating, the giant called for his magic harp. He told the harp to play, and it immediately began to play the most enchanting music Jack had ever heard.

Before long, the giant was lulled to sleep by the music. When Jack heard the giant begin to snore, he knew it was safe to climb out of the pot. He grabbed the harp and started to run away.

"Master! Master!" cried the harp. The giant awoke with a start. Jack jumped off the table with the harp in his arms, just as the giant made a grab for him. Jack held tightly onto the harp as he ran for his life. He raced out of the castle toward the magic beanstalk.

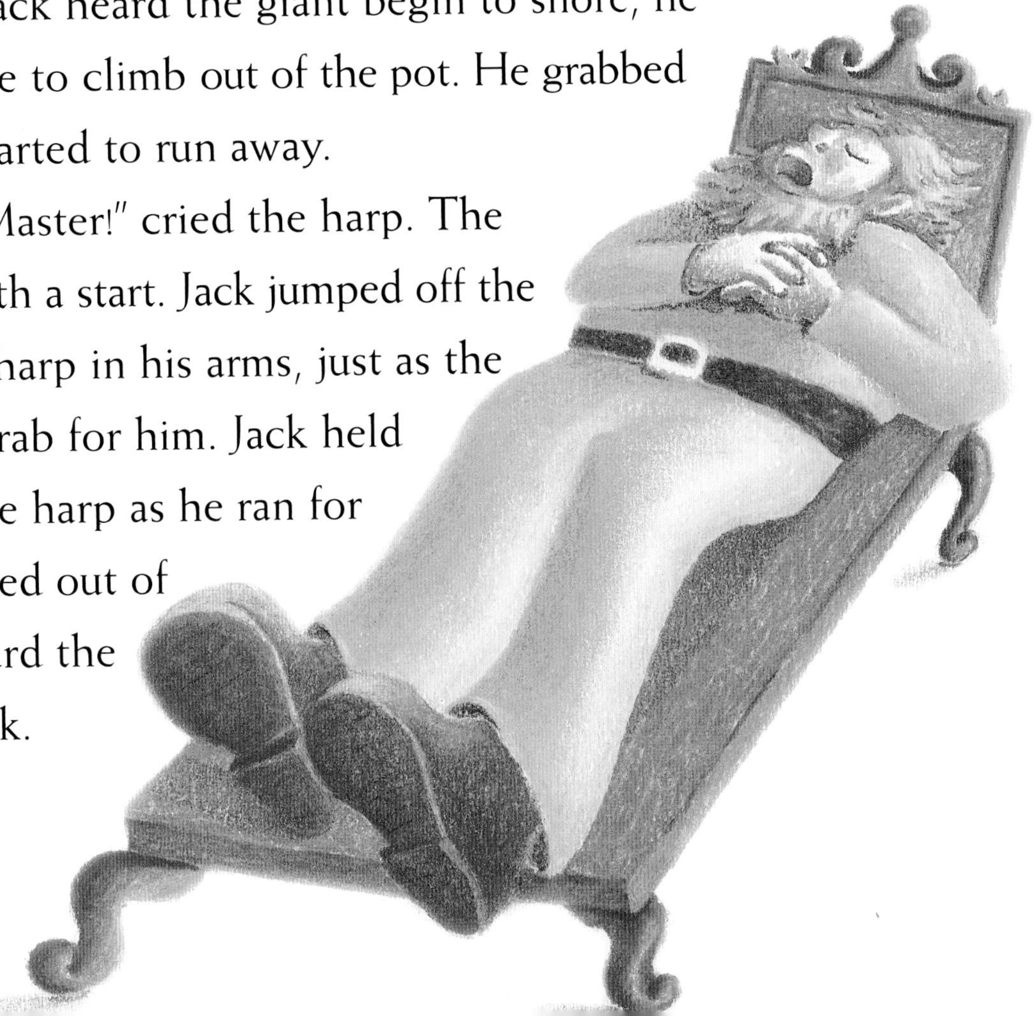

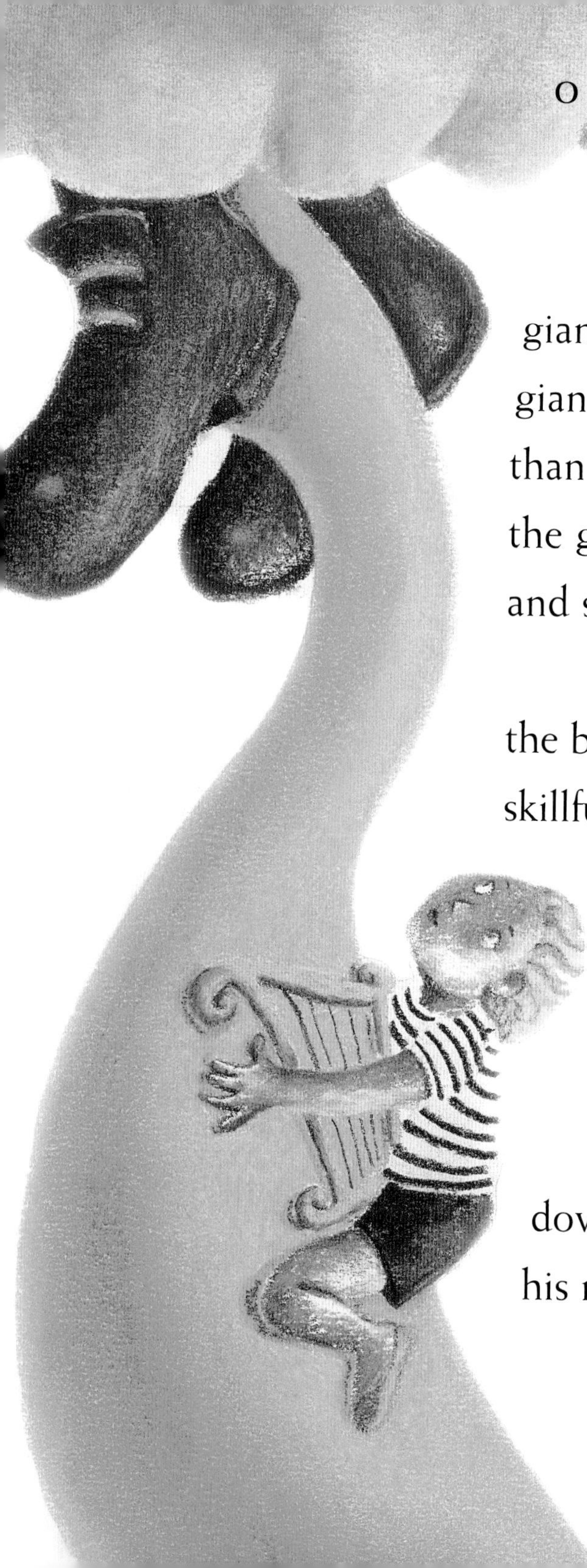

Jack could hear the *thump, thump* of the giant's footsteps behind him. He knew the giant took large steps, so Jack ran faster than he ever had before. Luckily for Jack, the giant had just finished a filling supper and so was rather slow on his feet.

By now, Jack was an expert at climbing the beanstalk. Even with the harp, he slid skillfully around stems and leaves. As Jack climbed down, he called to his mother.

"Mother! Hurry! Bring me the ax!" he shouted.

When Jack reached the ground, the giant was only halfway down the beanstalk. Jack took the ax from his mother and began to hack away.

Jack chopped at the beanstalk as fast as he could. The giant grew closer and closer to the ground until Jack made a mighty chop and cut the beanstalk in two. The giant and the beanstalk crashed to the ground.

Jack had successfully retrieved all of his father's treasure and saved everyone from the terrible giant in the clouds. Jack's mother was very proud of him. And the two of them, the hen, and the harp lived happily ever after.

The Nightingale

Adapted by Lisa Harkrader
Illustrated by Robin Moro

Many years ago, the emperor of China lived in a palace surrounded by beautiful gardens. Visitors came from all over the world to admire his silk draperies, exquisite vases, and rare flowers. But after the visitors had toured the palace and gardens, they were always eager to see more.

A local fisherman heard about the visitors' requests. He began taking them into the forest to see a beautiful nightingale that lived there. At first, people would simply grumble at the sight of the ordinary gray bird. It certainly did not look very remarkable.

But then the nightingale would open his mouth and sing.

Everyone who heard the nightingale's song agreed that it was lovelier than anything they had ever heard before.

Word quickly spread throughout the empire about the bird's beautiful singing. More people came to visit the palace and gardens. The nightingale became known to the people as the most beautiful thing in all of China. Everyone had heard of this remarkable bird.

Everyone, that is, except the emperor.

The emperor of China spent most of his time inside the palace. He did not know anything about the bird.

One day, the emperor received a letter from the emperor of Japan.

"I have heard about your wonderful nightingale," the Japanese emperor wrote. "I will arrive in two days to see the bird."

The Chinese emperor was puzzled. He summoned his prime minister. "Have you heard of this nightingale?" the emperor asked.

"No, Your Excellency," the prime minister said, scratching his chin.

"The emperor of Japan expects to see this bird," said the emperor. "Search until you find it."

The prime minister searched every inch of the palace, but he was unable find the nightingale.

He traveled deep into the woods but did not find the bird. He was about to give up hope when he came upon the fisherman. The fisherman knew exactly where to find the nightingale, and he led the prime minister right to him.

The prime minister returned to the palace with the bird.

Soon after, the emperor of Japan arrived in China for his visit.

"So this is the famous nightingale, the most beautiful thing in all of China," said the emperor of Japan. "I must say, he looks rather plain."

As soon as those words left the Japanese emperor's mouth, the nightingale began to sing. The emperor of Japan was speechless. The Chinese emperor cried tears of joy.

"I must find a way to thank you for allowing me to hear your nightingale's song," declared the emperor of Japan.

The Chinese emperor was very pleased with the lovely nightingale.

The nightingale remained in the palace, and day after day crowds of people came to hear his beautiful music.

Everyone loved the nightingale's song, but some visitors complained that the bird did not look as lovely as he sounded. Such comments made the emperor angry. The nightingale's song brought him such joy. He was happier than he had ever been before.

"I will not have people saying unkind words about the nightingale," he said.

So he gave the bird a golden perch to sit on, and he adorned the precious nightingale with ribbons and jewels. The people were delighted. Finally, the nightingale looked as beautiful as it sounded.

Each day the nightingale sat on its golden perch, wearing his jewels and singing for the visitors.

After a while, the little bird began to look tired and sad. The emperor brought the nightingale into his private chambers so the bird could sing to him at night.

"Gold and ribbons and fine jewels do not make your voice sound any lovelier," the emperor told him. "You are the finest thing in all of China when you are yourself, singing your sweet song."

The emperor drifted off to sleep each night to the sound of the nightingale's soft lullaby. The nightingale was very happy to sing peacefully in the emperor's chambers.

The nightingale and the emperor spent almost all of their time together. They grew to be close friends.

One day, a present arrived from the emperor of Japan.

"I hope you will enjoy this gift," wrote the Japanese emperor. "It is a small token compared with the great joy your nightingale's song gave to me."

The Chinese emperor carefully unwrapped the package from his friend. What could it be?

Inside, he found a replica of the nightingale. It was brightly colored and encrusted with exquisite green emeralds, blue sapphires, and red rubies. On its back was a sturdy key made of silver.

When the emperor wound the key, the mechanical bird began to sing. It was the same as one of the nightingale's songs!

It did not sound as lovely as the real nightingale, and it only sang one song, but still the emperor was pleased.

"Now you can rest," he told his beloved nightingale.

The people were thrilled with the mechanical bird.

"Finally! A nightingale that looks just as lovely as it sounds," they all said.

They did not notice that the jeweled bird's song was not as sweet as the real nightingale's song. They asked to hear the new nightingale over and over. Day and night, the palace was filled with visitors who wished to see the mechanical nightingale. Everyone ignored the real nightingale, so he flew home to the forest.

Only the emperor noticed that the nightingale had gone. He missed his friend deeply.

"It is for the best," the emperor said. "Surely the nightingale is happier in the forest."

Unlike the emperor, the people never grew tired of the mechanical bird's song. There was never a moment that the jeweled nightingale's song did not play. But one morning, with a loud twang and a pop, it stopped singing. The emperor wriggled the bird's key, but the bird would not sing. The emperor called for his watchmaker.

"A spring has broken," the watchmaker said. "I can replace it, but you will need to be careful. From now on, it may only be wound on special occasions."

The emperor grew ill. He missed the real nightingale. The prime minister and all the lords and ladies of the court tried their best, but they could not lift the emperor's spirits. Eventually, the old fisherman heard of the emperor's illness and went to find the nightingale.

After the fisherman's visit, the nightingale flew straight to the palace to see his friend the emperor.

The nightingale perched on the foot of the emperor's bed and began to sing his beautiful song.

The emperor opened his eyes.

"You came back," he whispered.

The emperor sat up in bed, and the color returned to his cheeks. The nightingale sang even more beautifully upon seeing the emperor's spirits rise.

After that day, the two friends never parted. The emperor cherished the nightingale for being himself, and he appreciated the great beauty of the bird's song. And the nightingale gladly sang his precious melodies in the peace of the emperor's palace.

Hansel and Gretel

Adapted by Suzanne Lieurance
Illustrated by Doug Klauba

Hansel and Gretel lived with their parents in a tiny cottage at the edge of the forest. Their father was a simple woodcutter, and although he worked hard, the family was very poor. Many times Hansel and Gretel had nothing but a crust of bread for their supper.

At night, after Hansel and Gretel were in bed, their parents would talk in worried voices. Even though they whispered, Hansel and Gretel could hear what they said.

"What is to become of us?" asked Father one night. "Soon we will not have enough money even for flour."

"We will manage," Mother said.

"I must go into the forest to find work," Father sighed. "Otherwise, we will surely starve."

Mother gasped. "There must be some other way," she replied anxiously. Then she calmed herself. "We will find one. Now, let's get some rest."

"Hansel, we can't let Father go," whispered Gretel to her brother from her bed. "What can we do?"

"I will travel into the forest, instead," replied Hansel.

"Then I will come with you," said Gretel bravely. "The forest is very dangerous. You may need my help."

"Very well," said Hansel. "We will leave tonight."

Before daylight, Hansel and Gretel crept out of their beds and pulled on their clothes. Gretel collected some bread from the kitchen and stuffed it into her pockets.

"I suppose it is not such a bad idea for you to come along," Hansel told Gretel as they took a last look at their house and began walking into the dark forest.

The children walked silently. They walked all day long through the tangled brush and tall trees. They walked until their feet hurt and their legs felt tired and heavy.

"I did not realize the forest was so big," Gretel said.

"Neither did I," said Hansel. "But don't worry. I have made sure we will not get lost. I left a trail of bread crumbs behind us, in case we need to turn back."

"You are very clever, Hansel," Gretel laughed.

"Why do you laugh?" Hansel asked. "I have sacrificed my bread to help us."

"Look!" Gretel said, pointing behind them. Three blackbirds hopped along, carefully eating each bread crumb Hansel had dropped. The trail Hansel had left for them had vanished completely.

"Hansel, here, eat some," Gretel said, trying to comfort her brother. She held out a piece of bread to him.

"I am not hungry anymore," Hansel said.

By now the children were very tired. They continued to walk through the forest. Surely they would come across someplace they could rest, or someone who could give them something small to eat. They were certainly lost now, and it felt as though they were walking in circles.

Night fell upon the forest, and strange noises came from behind the trees. Hansel and Gretel sat down and huddled against the cold.

"Did you hear that?" asked Hansel, reaching for Gretel's hand.

"It's only an owl," Gretel whispered. "We should try to sleep now."

Soon the children were asleep, dreaming of a warm supper.

In the morning they continued to walk. At first, to make the time pass, they sang songs that their parents had taught them. Soon they grew tired and hungry again and walked along in silence.

After a while, the children entered a small clearing. They could not believe their eyes.

"Gretel, look!" Hansel shouted. "A cottage!"

"Maybe whoever lives there will give us something to eat," said Gretel eagerly.

As the children hurried closer, they saw it was no ordinary cottage. Its walls were made of gingerbread, and the windows of clear sugar.

"It is the most beautiful house I have ever seen!" said Gretel.

"It is the most *delicious* house I have ever seen!" said Hansel, and he began to break off some frosting to eat.

"Wait!" Gretel cried. "We should see if anyone is home and ask before we eat."

The children knocked on the door. After a moment, it opened, and an old woman with a cane came out.

"Hello," the woman said sweetly.

"We have been traveling through the forest," Gretel said. "We are very tired and hungry. May we rest here?"

The old woman invited the children inside. She prepared them a meal of pancakes with rich syrup. Then she showed them to two beds that were covered with soft down.

But in the morning, as the children woke up, the old woman grabbed Hansel and locked him in a cage.

"She is a witch!" Hansel cried from inside the cage.

"That's right," the witch shouted. "I am a witch. And you will be my supper, once you are good and fat."

For the next few weeks, the witch made sure Hansel had plenty to eat. Gretel was given only crusts of bread. Each morning the witch would stand by Hansel's cage and say, "Stick out your finger so I can see how plump you are!"

But Hansel was clever. He knew that witches cannot see very well. Instead of his finger, he would stick out a thin little chicken bone that Gretel had managed to pass to him secretly.

"Hmmm," the witch would say, feeling the chicken bone. "What a scrawny thing you are! You must eat more!" Then the witch would yell at poor Gretel to bring Hansel more food.

One morning, the witch ordered Gretel to fetch some water. "Whether Hansel is fat or lean," she said, "today I will cook and eat him! I have waited long enough."

"No!" Gretel shouted.

"You stubborn child, do as I say," the witch demanded impatiently.

But Gretel would not move.

The witch nudged Gretel up to the oven. "Check the oven to make sure it is hot enough."

Gretel knew better than to trust the old witch.

"No," Gretel said. "I don't know how to check."

"Then I will do it myself!" shouted the witch. She shoved Gretel aside. Then she hobbled over to the oven and poked her head inside.

Just as she did, Gretel gave her a push. The witch fell right into the oven. Gretel quickly slammed the iron door and bolted it so the old witch could not get out.

"I told you that you would need my help," Gretel said as she opened the door of Hansel's cage. Hansel sprang out and hugged her.

With nothing else to fear, the children sat down and enjoyed a feast of cookies, fresh bread, and candies.

Before they left the cottage, the children gathered food to eat during their long journey home.

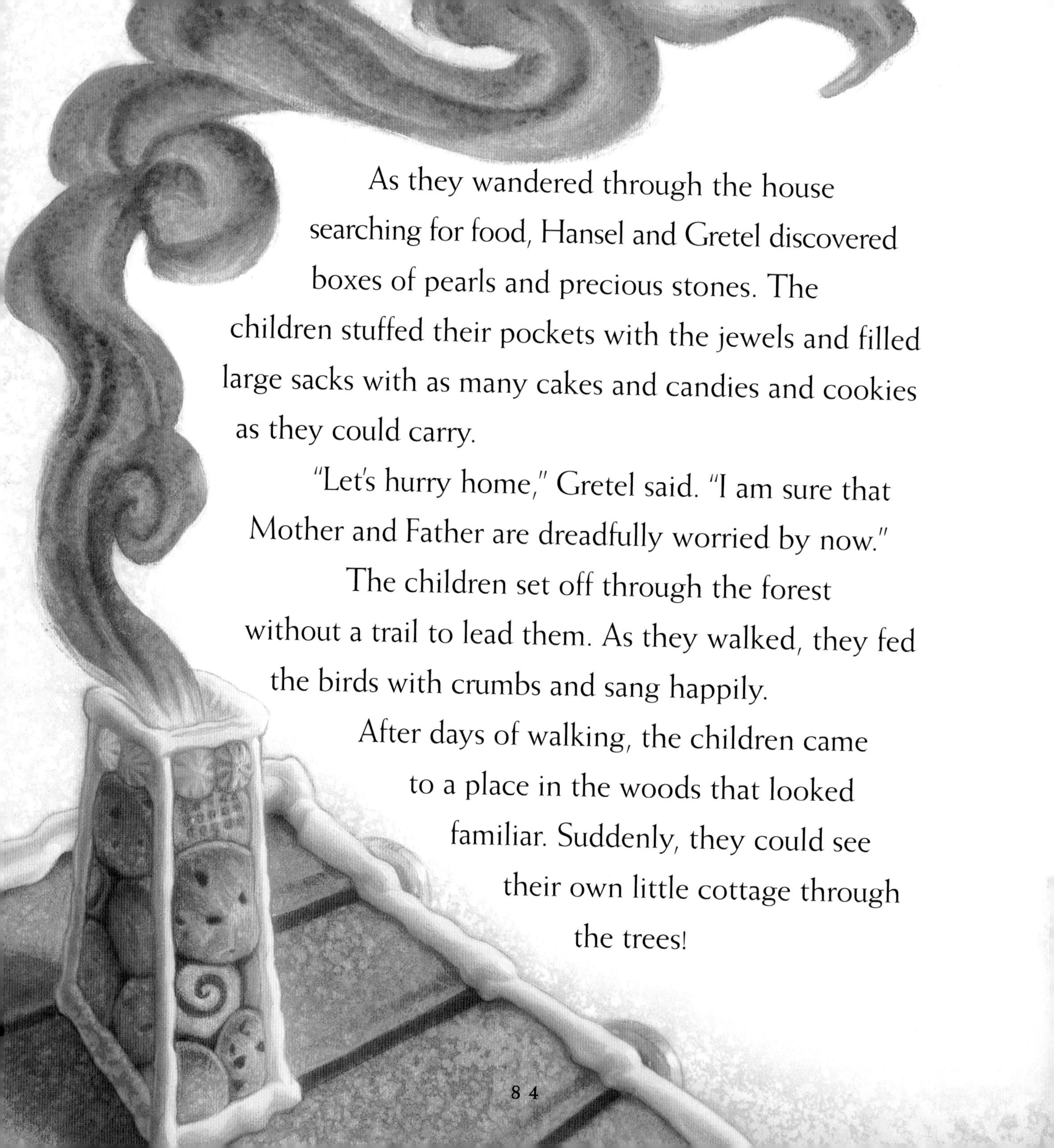

As they wandered through the house searching for food, Hansel and Gretel discovered boxes of pearls and precious stones. The children stuffed their pockets with the jewels and filled large sacks with as many cakes and candies and cookies as they could carry.

"Let's hurry home," Gretel said. "I am sure that Mother and Father are dreadfully worried by now."

The children set off through the forest without a trail to lead them. As they walked, they fed the birds with crumbs and sang happily.

After days of walking, the children came to a place in the woods that looked familiar. Suddenly, they could see their own little cottage through the trees!

The children began to run.

"Mother, Father! We are home at last!" they shouted joyfully.

When Mother and Father heard their calls, they ran to meet them. They hugged Hansel and Gretel for a very long time.

"Look what we have brought," said Hansel. He took the jewels from his pockets and laid them on the table. "We will never be hungry again."

"You are very good children," said Father, "and very brave. But you must promise me that you will never go into the forest again, for it is a very dangerous place."

Hansel and Gretel looked at each other and smiled.

"We promise," they said together.

Sleeping Beauty

Adapted by Charles Sharp
Illustrated by Holly Jones

There was once a beloved queen who, after many childless years, gave birth to a beautiful daughter. The queen's loyal subjects prepared a festival to welcome the baby princess.

Deep in a dark forest of the same kingdom, there lived a wicked witch who led a lonely life. "Bah!" cried the bitter witch. "I'll put a stop to all these cheers!"

With evil in her heart, the witch set out for the castle. The moment she arrived, the cruel witch cast a terrible spell on the princess.

"On the princess's sixteenth birthday," hissed the witch, "she will prick her finger. This will cause her to fall into a deep sleep . . . from which she will never awaken!"

The queen gasped. Holding her baby close, she whispered, "I promise to do my best to keep you safe."

Sixteen years later, the princess prepared for her birthday party. She noticed a tiny rip in her dress and decided to mend it herself. But as she stitched, the princess pricked her finger on the sharp needle. As the witch had predicted, the princess at once fell into a deep sleep.

The queen was horrified to find her daughter fast asleep on the floor of the sewing room. She knew at once what had happened. The princess was brought to her own room and put to bed.

The devastated queen summoned all of the best doctors, witches, and warlocks to the castle, but they were unable to reverse the spell.

One day, a fairy arrived at the castle to see the sleeping princess. The fairy sat with the girl for a long time, whispering comforting words in her ear.

"I have news about your daughter," the fairy told the queen. In her travels, the fairy had met a bitter old witch who bragged about her powerful spells. The sneering witch had mentioned the one thing that could break her formidable sleeping spell.

"True love," the fairy told the queen. "If a man of pure heart falls in love with the princess, she will awaken from her sleep."

"What man would fall in love with a sleeping girl?" asked the queen, sighing. "All hope is surely lost."

"I cannot awaken your daughter," said the fairy solemnly. "The witch's magic is too powerful. But there is something I can do."

"To bring you comfort," continued the fairy, "I can cast a spell on you and your subjects, so that you may all share the princess's slumber. When the princess awakens, so too will you."

The queen sat deep in thought. "I agree to this plan," she answered, finally. "Now, kind fairy, cast your spell on me and my people."

As quickly as an eyelid flutters shut, the queen and everyone else in the castle settled into a deep sleep.

Over the years, the castle courtyards became overgrown. After a hundred years had passed, a dense forest had grown around the silent castle.

One day a young, handsome prince was riding his horse through the forest. In a thicket of brambles, he glimpsed a stone wall. Cautiously, the prince went closer.

"A hidden castle!" he exclaimed. The prince cleared away vines and found a doorway. Then he noticed that at his feet lay a guard, sound asleep. When the guard would not awaken, the prince decided to enter the castle and investigate.

The prince walked through a great hall, finding more sleeping people with every step. "Wake up!" he shouted, but it was no use. Everyone slept soundly.

Soon the prince came to the princess's room. "She is beautiful," he whispered in awe.

The prince gazed at her face, so peaceful and lovely. Overcome with emotion, the prince stepped to the girl's bedside. He lifted her hand and gently kissed it.

At the prince's kiss, the princess's eyes opened in a flash. She looked with wide eyes at the young man sitting beside her.

"It's you!" she said. "You have come to me at last! I waited for you in my dream. A kind fairy told me you would come!"

At the same moment the princess awakened, so did the queen and her sleeping subjects.

The queen rushed to the princess's room.

"My daughter!" she said, overjoyed. "You have come back to me!"

The queen looked at the prince. He was the man of pure heart whom the fairy had described.

"Thank you," she said, embracing him. "You have saved my daughter and my kingdom!"

As the people throughout the castle woke from their long slumber, they rubbed the sleep of a hundred years from their eyes. The queen's joyful cries soon reached their ears. Everyone hurried to see the princess. "Our princess is awake!" they cheered, already celebrating.

The queen introduced her subjects to the prince.

"This man loves my daughter," said the queen, "and they will be married as soon as possible. We have waited a long time for this day. Let us not waste another moment!"

In a few short days, the sound of wedding bells rang throughout the kingdom. The prince and princess were married in the grandest ceremony imaginable.

The prince, his heart filled with love, had never been happier. The princess had truly found the man of her dreams, and they lived happily ever after.

Three Golden Flowers

Adapted by Lisa Harkrader
Illustrated by Marty Noble

Once there was a chief who ruled an island tribe. He lived a happy life until one day his daughter became very ill. The chief called for the tribe's healers. The healers did everything they could for the princess; they gave her herbs, bathed her in oils, and burned spices to soothe her.

But the princess continued to grow weaker. Soon she could barely lift her head from her pillow. The chief was deeply concerned, and he sent for the tribal wise man.

"Find three golden orchids," the wise man said upon examining the princess. "Their scent will cure her."

"Where are these golden flowers?" asked the chief.

"They grow only where the sun shines through the water," said the wise man.

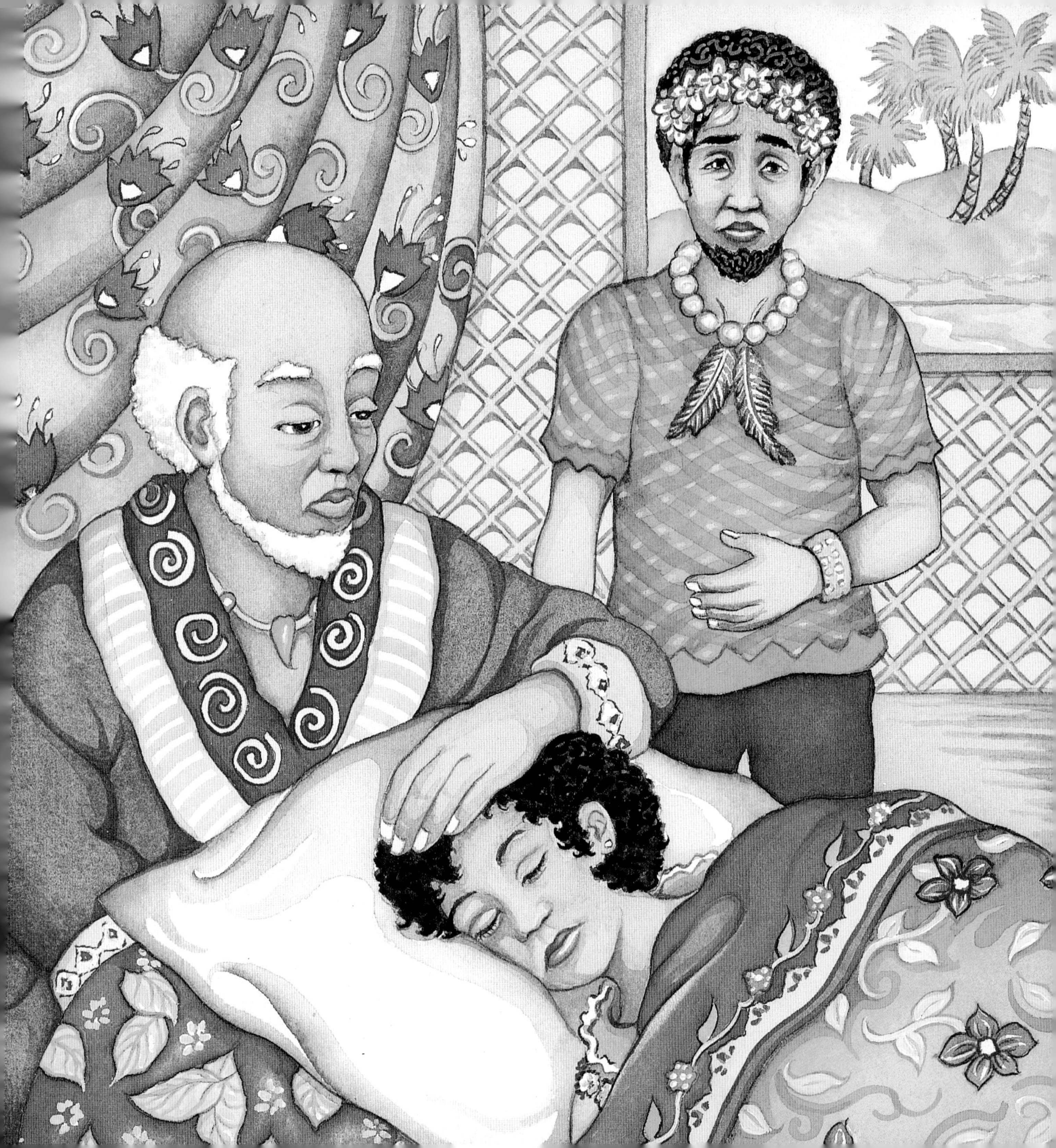

The chief proclaimed that any man who could bring him the three golden orchids could marry the princess.

The great warriors of the tribe, eager to earn the princess's hand in marriage, explored every inch of the island. But they could not find any golden orchids.

On a nearby island, a poor man lived with his wife and three sons. The sons were not great warriors; they were modest farmers, like their father.

When the family heard the chief's proclamation, they were excited. They knew exactly where to find the flowers that would cure the princess. Each year, nine perfect orchids—delicate and golden—grew behind a waterfall in a hidden valley.

The oldest of the brothers went to the valley and picked the three largest orchids. He placed them carefully in a basket and set off in his canoe across the sea.

When the eldest brother reached the chief's island, he met an old fisherman on the beach.

"What have you there?" asked the fisherman.

The young man knew that everyone was searching for the orchids. He was afraid the old man would steal the basket if he knew what treasure lay inside.

"Fishing worms," the young man said.

The fisherman smiled and allowed him to continue.

The young man reached the village, and soon he stood before the chief. When he opened his basket, he was surprised to find worms, just as he had told the fisherman.

When the eldest brother returned home, the middle brother decided to try his luck. He, too, met the fisherman on the beach. Like his older brother, he was suspicious and lied to the fisherman. Later, when he met the chief, he also found his basket filled with worms.

Now only three golden orchids remained. The youngest brother picked them and set off to see the chief.

He, too, met the fisherman. Again, the fisherman asked what was in the basket. But this boy was honest with him. "I carry flowers that will cure the princess," he said.

"Indeed you do," said the fisherman. Then he gave the boy a bamboo flute. "It will bring you luck," he said.

The boy thanked the fisherman and ran to the village. At first, the wary chief refused to see him. But the boy opened his basket to reveal the golden orchids. They were as perfect as when he had first picked them.

As soon as the princess smelled the orchids, her eyes opened. She looked up and smiled. She thanked the boy, and soon the two were laughing and talking together.

The chief was pleased that his daughter was cured, but he did not want the princess to marry the son of a farmer.

"You have cured my daughter," he told the boy, "but now you must prove that you are worthy to marry her. Tomorrow, you must take a hundred parrots into the forest. In the evening, you must bring them all back safely. If any are missing, you cannot marry my daughter."

The boy spent the next day chasing the parrots, but by nightfall, he could not find a single one. Suddenly, he remembered the lucky bamboo flute. He trilled a few notes, and all of the parrots flew to him.

When the young man returned with all one hundred parrots, the chief could not believe his eyes.

"If my daughter will have you," said the chief humbly, "then I will welcome you into our family."

When they were older, the princess did indeed marry this boy. They lived happily ever after on the island.

George and the Dragon

Adapted by Brian Conway
Illustrated by Tammie Speer Lyon

This is the tale of George and the dragon, a story that has been told for more than fifteen centuries. It takes place during a time called the Dark Ages, when kings ruled the land, wizards cast spells, and monsters roamed free.

The story begins in the land of fairies. The queen of the fairies had taken in young George when he was abandoned as a baby. The fairies raised George to be brave and strong. They taught him to be a noble knight, skilled with a sword, but even more skilled with his mind.

In time, the queen of the fairies called George to see her. It was time for George to seek his destiny.

"Your journey begins today," she told him. "You will have many adventures ahead, to be sure. You should not expect an easy path. Life is seldom easy."

The queen of the fairies spoke kindly to young George. "The world is filled with monsters and battles. You will meet kings and paupers, wizards and witches, evil princes and kind princesses," she said. "As you travel, you must always remember one thing," the queen added, tapping George's silver battle helmet. "Your greatest weapon is your brain."

Then George set off. He traveled for weeks. As he approached a town called Silene, he noticed the land had changed from lush and green to dark and desolate. It seemed the ground had been crossed by fire. There was no grass, only the darkest mud. The trees were bare and black, and a foul stench filled the air.

George made his way through the bleak landscape until he saw a castle in the distance. A high, solid wall surrounded the castle and the small city around it. The gate was closed up tight.

A beautiful woman approached George.

"You must leave here," she warned. "It isn't safe!"

"But I am a brave knight, here to help you," George said. "It is my destiny. I will assist you at all costs."

"Alas, sir," the woman replied, "you are but one man. I fear that you cannot help."

"I will not leave," said George. "Please, let me try."

"I am Princess Sabra," she said. "Come with me."

Sabra explained why the kingdom lived in such fear. A wicked dragon lived in the caves of the nearby forest, she told him. The horrible beast was ravaging the land and eating all of the animals.

The princess explained that when the dragon finished eating the animals, he would certainly look for a new source of food. When that happened, the townspeople were in danger of becoming the dragon's next meal.

"There must be something we can do," George said.

Sabra told George of a cave in the dark forest where a wise old hermit lived. She thought that he might be able to help. They found the cave and entered quietly. Sabra and George crept up to the old hermit, who stared into his fire. He did not look at them, but he began to chant:

Long ago, it was told,
Two brave souls would come to know
The only way to save the rest:
The Serpent's weakness is in his breath.

With those words, an hourglass appeared at their feet. They were puzzled, but the hermit would speak no more.

George and Sabra left the cave. They knew they must hurry to the dragon's lair. They had to get there while the dragon slept. It was their only chance.

"The hermit speaks in puzzles," Sabra sighed. "What will we do with this ancient timepiece?"

George studied the hourglass. "The hourglass will lead us," George whispered. "We must wait until all the sand has dropped through."

George and Sabra found their way to the lair. The dragon was asleep as they entered, but not for long.

Suddenly, the dragon stirred. It stood and rubbed its eyes. George watched as the very last grain of sand dropped through the hourglass. The glass turned icy cold.

At that moment, the dragon yawned a great, fiery yawn. George knew this was his chance. He threw the hourglass into the dragon's mouth!

The hourglass broke apart on the dragon's tongue in a cloud of icy mist.

The dragon was furious! He looked down to see George and Sabra. Then he stretched out his body before rearing back to hurl a fiery blast at them. To the great relief of George and Sabra, but to the horror of the dragon, only soft snow came from the great beast's mouth.

The dragon took a deep breath and tried again, but his mouth was suddenly frozen—shut tight with ice. The hourglass had been filled with magical, icy sand. The dragon jumped into the deep, warm lake to keep from freezing from the inside out.

That dragon never bothered another soul. Some have seen him come up for air on occasion, but only on very warm nights. The dragon would not dare stay out of the warm water too long, for fear of becoming an icy statue.

George and Sabra had saved the kingdom!

News of the dragon's defeat traveled back to the village. When George and Sabra returned, they were greeted with cries of joy and triumph. The grateful people of Silene were no longer prisoners in their own kingdom.

The king offered George bags of gold in thanks, but George wanted no payment for his deeds.

"I have set out in this world to face many adventures and adversities," George told the people. "Knowing that I was able to provide a service to those in need is reward enough for me."

George continued on his journey. The legend of his bravery preceded him, but with every stop along the way, he added to the story with continued acts of bravery. Villages far and wide came to know George as the brave and noble knight that he was raised to be.

The Princess and the Pea

Adapted by Michael P. Fertig
Illustrated by Anthony Lewis

In a land so far away that it would take as long to travel there from one direction as from another, there lived a young prince named Horatio. Prince Horatio was much admired for being kind and loyal, as well as smart, brave, and handsome. In short, he was a perfect prince. And as if that was not enough, he was also quite a stylish dresser.

All of the ladies in town wanted to marry Prince Horatio. It was well-known throughout his kingdom that the prince was searching for a bride. But it was also well-known that his mother was very particular about whom she would allow her son to marry. Any woman who wished to wed Prince Horatio must be a princess, through and through.

"There are so many princesses these days," said the prince's mother. "But only a real princess with a kind, generous, and delicate nature will be good enough for my dear Horatio."

The prince was bothered by his mother's wish for him to find the perfect bride. But in truth, none of the princesses he had met held much interest for him. He simply had not yet met the girl of his dreams.

On this particular dark and rainy evening, however, all of that was about to change. The prince was just getting ready to turn in for the night when there was a knock at the castle door.

"Forgive me for the intrusion," said a lovely young woman. "But my carriage has lost a wheel in the road. Could I impose upon you for shelter this evening?"

"Of course," replied the prince. "Please come in."

"Thank you very much," she said. "My name is Astrid. I am a princess from Wainscott, just over the hills."

The prince led Princess Astrid to the castle's parlor where a fire was burning in the hearth, and the two sat down together. They immediately fell into conversation and talked well into the night. Before they realized it, the prince and the princess were holding each other's hands.

Elsewhere in the castle, the prince's mother had devised a plan to determine whether Astrid was a real princess. It is a little-known fact, but a real princess has such a delicate nature that she can detect even the slightest flaw in otherwise comfortable sleeping arrangements. So the queen hid a single uncooked pea underneath a stack of twenty of the softest mattresses in the kingdom. A true princess—one who lived up to the queen's standards—would certainly be able to detect the pea.

Astrid was shown to her room. She climbed atop the twenty mattresses, hoping to dream of Prince Horatio. But sleep would not come. Aware that something was not right, Astrid climbed down and slipped her arm beneath the bottom mattress. She pulled out the pea and said, "Aha! Just as I thought. Now for some rest."

In the morning, the queen asked how Astrid had slept.

"I was quite uncomfortable at first," Astrid admitted. "But then I discovered a pea under the mattresses. After I removed it, I slept very well."

The prince and his mother exchanged glances. In a flash, Prince Horatio was on his knee, proposing to beautiful Princess Astrid. Much to the dismay of the unwed ladies of the kingdom, Princess Astrid accepted. The couple remains happily married to this very day.

The Selfish Giant

Adapted by William E. Driscol
Illustrated by David Lupton

Once there was a beautiful garden. It was covered with grass that was as soft and cool as a pillow. Scattered about the garden were colorful flowers and peach trees that wore pink blossoms in spring and bore plump fruit in fall. Birds filled the sweet garden with their melodies. They seemed to call, "Children, come to our garden and play!"

And come the children did. Each day, on their way home from school, the children would visit the garden. They would lie in the cool grass and hide among the trees. They would pick flowers for their mothers and eat the sweet peaches for a snack. How happy they were!

KEEP
OUT!

But one day, the giant returned. This was his garden, but he had been away for seven years, visiting his cousin the ogre. When he arrived, he saw the children playing in his garden.

"What are you doing here?" he cried in a gruff voice. "This is *my* garden. Nobody can play here but me!"

To make his point clear, the giant locked the gate and nailed two sturdy planks of wood across the doorway. Then he hung a sign that said: "Keep Out!"

The children watched the giant sadly.

Now the children had nowhere to play. They tried playing on the road, but it was too dusty. They tried playing outside their school, but they were shooed away after their lessons. Each day, the children would walk around the high garden wall and remember the fun they used to have inside.

Soon, spring turned to summer, and summer became fall. Then fall gave way to winter. When winter said farewell, spring came again. Everywhere the land was filled with birds and blossoms. Everywhere, that is, except the selfish giant's garden.

The birds refused to sing there, since no children would hear their songs. The trees refused to blossom, since no children would climb their branches and taste their sweet, ripe fruit.

And so snow covered the grass with her white cloak, and frost painted all of the trees silver. The wind hissed through the garden, blowing its icy breath.

"I cannot understand why spring is so late in coming," said the giant, as he looked out at his cold, white garden. "I hope it will come soon."

But spring never came, nor summer.

One morning, the giant was lying in bed when he heard some lovely music. It sounded so sweet to his ears that he thought it was the king's musicians. But it was really a bluebird singing outside his window. It was so long since he had heard a bird sing in his garden that it seemed to him the most beautiful music in the world.

The selfish giant sat up and looked out the window. What do you think he saw?

It was a most wonderful sight. The children had crept into the garden through a hole in the wall. The trees were so happy to have them back again that they had covered themselves with pink and white blossoms.

The giant's heart melted as he looked out.

"How selfish I have been!" he cried. "Now I know why spring would not come."

He was very sorry for what he had done.

The giant crept downstairs and slowly opened the door. As he entered the garden, he saw that in one corner it was still winter. A little boy stood beneath a tree, stretching his arms up to reach its high branches. The poor tree was still quite covered with frost, and although it bent its branches as low as it could, the boy was too small to climb them.

The giant smiled at the little boy and lifted him gently into the tree. At once, the tree broke into bloom, and birds perched on its branches and sang. The little boy smiled shyly at the giant.

"Does this mean we may play in your garden?" asked the little boy.

"From now on, this is your garden," answered the giant. "You and your friends may come and play here whenever you wish."

The giant took his great ax and opened the garden gate once more. From that day forward, the gate was never closed again.

Every day, the children returned to play in the lovely place. They brought their friends and their sisters and brothers. It truly became a place for all children.

When the giant opened the gate to his garden, he opened his heart as well. He finally understood that it was the children who made the garden a magical place.

Being selfish had made the giant lonely. But when he learned to share, friends filled his garden and happiness filled his heart.

Each afternoon, the giant could be seen laughing and playing games with the children. The trees continued to bloom, and the birds sang in the garden with all their hearts. Everyone lived happily ever after.

The Ugly Duckling

Adapted by Sarah Toast
Illustrated by Susan Spellman

One fine summer day, a mother duck watched her eggs begin to hatch. "You are the sweetest little yellow ducklings!" she cried proudly. "Are you all here?"

But the biggest egg had not yet hatched.

The mother duck settled back down on the final egg and waited. After a time, that shell, too, began to crack. And out tumbled a clumsy gray duckling.

This duckling was larger than the others and very ugly.

The mother duck considered him carefully. "He is a most enormous duckling," she thought to herself. "And he looks nothing like the others. I wonder if he can swim. We shall see tomorrow."

The mother duck quacked to her babies to follow, and they waddled to the barnyard.

"My," said a goose in the barnyard, "that gray fellow looks awfully big for his age."

The gray duckling stayed close to his mother. She ignored the goose's rude remarks and continued on her way.

The next day the sun shone brightly. The mother duck led her ducklings down to the pond.

"Quack, quack," she told them. "Do what I do."

One after another, the eager ducklings hopped into the blue water. They bobbed and floated like little corks. They already seemed to know how to paddle their legs and swim! All of the new ducklings swam very nicely.

The ugly duckling was an especially good swimmer. The mother duck was very pleased with all her ducklings, and she decided to take them out to the meadow.

"Follow me! Waddle this way, and say 'Quack,'" she instructed her brood. "Don't turn in your toes!"

The little ducklings did as their mother did. But the gray duckling was clumsy. The tall meadow grass made him trip and fall.

His brothers and sisters laughed at the gray duckling.

"Why can't you walk like us?" they asked. "And why do you look so different from us? Are you certain you are our brother?"

The poor ugly duckling hid his head under his wing. How sad he was! He did not know what made him so different from his brothers and sisters. He only wanted to be loved.

At last, the ugly duckling could stand no more teasing. He decided to run away and go to a place where no one knew him.

The little duckling passed the pond, and then the barnyard, and finally the meadow. He traveled until he came to a large marsh, where he chose to spend the night.

In the morning, the little duckling was greeted by some wild geese who lived there.

"What sort of creature are you?" the geese asked him, not unkindly. "You don't look like us, but that is all right. You may stay with us for now."

But just then, a hunter's dog walked by. The geese were startled and flew away. The frightened duckling remained very still, hiding behind the marsh grass for as long as he could. When he was certain the dog was gone, the little duckling set off again across the meadow.

Soon the duckling came to a crooked little hut. Its wooden door stood open, and he waddled inside.

An old woman lived in the hut with her cat and her hen. Being rather blind, the old woman thought the duck might lay some duck eggs for her. And so she let him stay.

The poor little duckling could not purr like the cat or lay eggs like the hen. The animals teased him mercilessly.

"What good are you?" they asked him. And the duckling could not say.

The teasing made the duckling miss the pond and the wonderful feeling of swimming. So he left the crooked little hut.

The duckling found a small lake where he could dive to the bottom and pop back up again to float in the water. The wild ducks who lived there ignored him because he was so ugly.

Autumn came, and with it, clouds and cold winds. One evening at sunset, a flock of beautiful birds with huge, powerful wings flew overhead. Their feathers were shining white, and they had long, graceful necks and smart black noses. The beauty of the swans—for that is what they were—made the ugly duckling long to follow them.

The weather grew colder. It became so cold that one day the lake froze around the duckling. Luckily, a farmer came along and freed him from the ice. He tucked the duckling under his arm and carried him home.

The farmer's children were excited to play with the duckling. But he thought they were going to hurt him. In his fright he ran into a milk pail. Then he flapped into a barrel of flour.

The farmer's wife was horrified when she saw the mess he had made. She chased the duckling out of the house and into the cold snow.

The children followed the ugly duckling and tried to catch him, but he found a hiding place under some bushes. As the snow fell silently around him, he lay still until the children went back indoors.

The ugly duckling had a difficult winter. Food was scarce, and the frosty winds howled across the meadow. He noticed that his feathers had begun to fall out. The duckling used them to line the nest he had built beneath a snowdrift. He imagined that without his feathers, he must be even uglier than before.

When spring finally arrived, the warm sun shone. The grass became soft and green, and the song of birds and the fragrance of new flowers filled the air.

Filled with the joy of spring, the duckling spread his wings to fly. My, how strong his wings had become!

Below, he saw three swans floating on a lake. The ugly duckling suddenly longed to be near them. He landed on the water and swam toward them.

As the ugly duckling drew near, he bowed his head, expecting to be taunted by the lovely creatures. When he looked down, he saw another graceful swan floating on the lake. It was his own reflection!

He was no longer a clumsy, ugly duckling. He was a swan. His ugly gray feathers had dropped away, and now his feathers were white and shiny. He had powerful wings and a long and graceful neck.

"I am beautiful, like you," he whispered to the swans.

The swans encircled him and stroked him with their beaks. Finally, the ugly duckling knew where he belonged.

Goldilocks and the Three Bears

Adapted by Caleb Burroughs
Illustrated by David Merrell

In the heart of a great forest, there once sat a cozy, comfortable cottage. In this cottage lived a family of bears: Papa Bear, Mama Bear, and wee Baby Bear.

The three bears began each morning the same way. They made their beds, tidied their house, and ate their breakfast together at the table.

One particular morning, Mama Bear made a breakfast of piping-hot porridge. The porridge was so piping hot, in fact, that the three bears decided to take a walk through the forest while their breakfast cooled.

This very same morning, a young girl named Goldilocks came upon the cottage.

"Mmmm," said the girl, "I believe I smell fresh porridge! Why, perhaps I will sneak into this cottage and have just a bite or two."

Now, it isn't very nice to go inside someone's cottage when no one is at not home. And it isn't very nice to nibble at someone's porridge without asking. But this is exactly what Goldilocks did.

She took a bite of Papa Bear's porridge, but it was too hot. She took a bite of Mama Bear's porridge, but it was too cold. Then she took a bite of Baby Bear's porridge, and it was so good that she ate it all!

Her belly full, Goldilocks needed to rest for a bit. Finding the bears' chairs, Goldilocks decided to sit down.

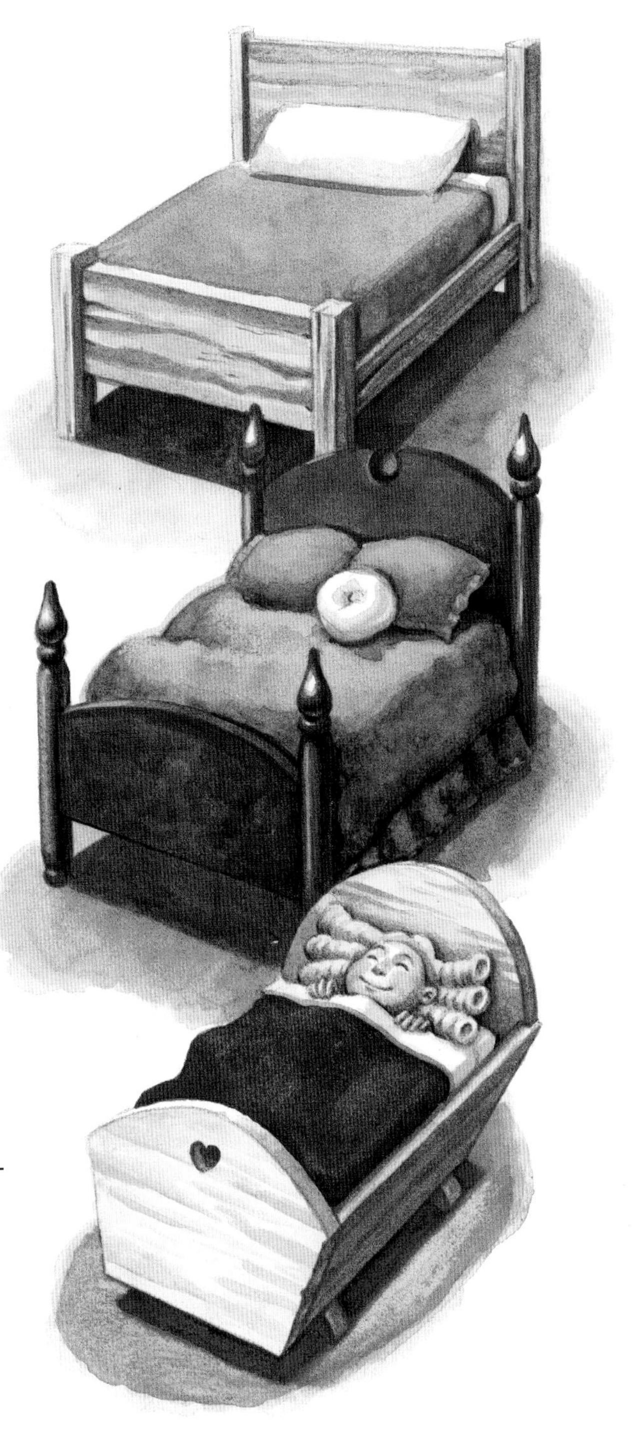

Goldilocks sat down on Papa Bear's chair, but it was too hard. She sat on Mama Bear's chair, but it was too soft. Then she sat down on Baby Bear's chair, and it was just right—until it broke with a loud *SNAP!*

Needing somewhere new to nap, Goldilocks found the bears' newly made beds. She tried Papa Bear's bed, but it was too firm. She tried Mama Bear's bed, but it was too squishy. Then she snuggled into Baby Bear's bed, which was just right—so right that she soon fell asleep.

At about the same time that Goldilocks was drifting off to sleep in Baby Bear's bed, the bear family was finishing their brisk morning walk. Certain that their porridge would be cool enough to eat, Papa Bear, Mama Bear, and Baby Bear sat down at the table for breakfast.

Papa Bear was the first to pick up his spoon and look down at his porridge. What he saw did not please him.

"Hmmm," Papa Bear growled, letting his spoon drop to the table. "It seems that someone has been eating my porridge!"

"Oh, don't be silly," replied Mama Bear. She then picked up her spoon, in order to try her own bowl of porridge.

"Heavens to Betsy!" muttered Mama Bear, putting her napkin to her mouth. "It seems that someone has been eating my porridge, too!"

It isn't every day that one finds one's breakfast has been eaten by someone else. But this did not matter to Baby Bear, who had become quite hungry from taking such a long morning walk. It was as if he hadn't heard his mother or father complain about their porridge.

"Oh, dear!" Baby Bear cried as he looked at his bowl. "It seems that someone has been eating my porridge—and has eaten it all up!"

Sure enough, Baby Bear's little bowl was as empty as his stomach. It had been licked clean, with not a dab of porridge to be found at all.

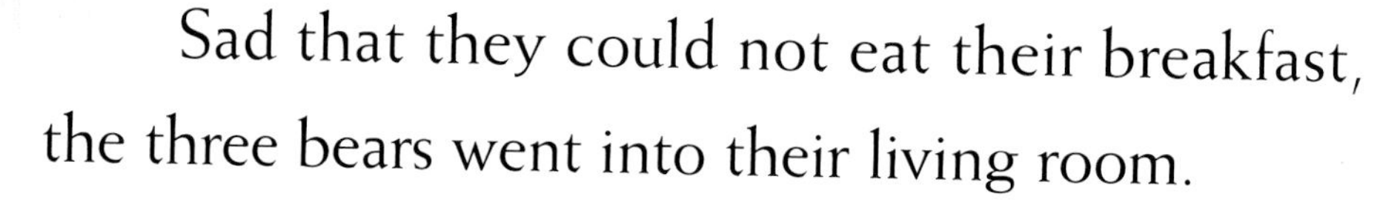

Sad that they could not eat their breakfast, the three bears went into their living room.

"Let's all calm down," said Mama Bear. Papa Bear went to his big, hard wooden chair and sat down, but something wasn't right.

"What?" he roared, jumping up from his seat. "It seems that someone has been sitting in my chair!"

"Now, dear, don't be silly," said Mama Bear calmly. "I'm sure your chair is fine."

With that, Mama Bear sat down in her soft, comfortable chair—and arose with a start.

"Fiddlesticks!" she declared. "It seems that someone has been sitting in my chair, too!"

Baby Bear was still forlorn from finding his porridge all eaten up. He was so forlorn, in fact, that he didn't hear his parents' complaints. With a frown and a pout, he flopped onto the spot where his small chair had been.

"Eek!" Baby Bear squealed. "It seems that someone has been sitting in my little chair—and has smashed it all to bits and pieces!"

Sure enough, Mama Bear and Papa Bear looked down to find poor Baby Bear's special chair lying broken on the floor.

Now not only had the bears' breakfast been ruined, but so had their living room. Not knowing what else to do, the tired and worried bears went to their bedrooms.

Papa Bear was the first to climb into his bed.

"Whoa!" he shouted, jumping from under the covers. "It seems that someone has been sleeping in my bed!"

"Nonsense," said Mama Bear, climbing into her own bed. "You must be imagining things."

But no sooner had Mama gotten under the covers than she arose yelping, "Well, it seems that someone has been sleeping in my bed, too!"

Baby Bear had now gone to his own bed.

"Help!" cried Baby Bear. "It seems that someone has been sleeping in my bed—and she's still here!"

Sure enough, the three bears spotted the small, blond-haired girl napping in Baby Bear's bed. As the bears stared at Goldilocks, she woke up. When Goldilocks saw the three large bears looking down at her, she was so frightened that she leaped out of the window!

Goldilocks never went back into that part of the forest again. And she never ate another bite of oatmeal.

Vasilissa and the Magic Doll

Adapted by Sarah Toast
Illustrated by Nan Brooks

Long ago in faraway Russia, there lived a merchant, his wife, and their young daughter, Vasilissa.

Sadly, Vasilissa's mother became ill.

"Beloved daughter," Vasilissa's mother said, "I am dying. But do not worry. I have made you a doll to keep with you always. You must not tell anyone about her."

Vasilissa took the doll and slipped it into her pocket.

"Whenever you are afraid or sad," said her mother, "give the doll a bit to eat and drink. Then tell her your troubles. She will tell you what to do."

Vasilissa kissed her mother.

"Bless you, child, and do not cry," said her mother. "I will always be with you." Then she closed her eyes.

Vasilissa tried not to cry. She reached for her doll and gave her a tiny piece of bread and a drop of milk. She whispered, "I am sad because I miss my mother."

Vasilissa heard a tiny voice say, "Do not cry, little Vasilissa. Go to sleep. The morning is wiser than the evening." Vasilissa curled up in her little bed and fell asleep.

One day, Vasilissa's father returned home from a trip with a new wife. She had two older daughters who were jealous of Vasilissa's beauty. Vasilissa's stepmother was as cruel as Vasilissa was kind. She dealt very harshly with Vasilissa.

The stepmother and her daughters made Vasilissa do all of the work in the house. They sat like queens, while Vasilissa scrubbed and chopped, cooked and cleaned.

Every night, Vasilissa would take her doll from her pocket. She would feed the doll and whisper her troubles in her tiny ear. The doll would always comfort Vasilissa.

When Vasilissa's father left on a trip to buy goods, the cruel stepmother devised a plan to get rid of Vasilissa.

That night, the stepmother secretly blew out the only candle the family left burning at night.

"What shall we do?" cried the stepmother. "There is no light! Vasilissa, you must go to the witch Baba Yaga and ask her for a flame!" She pushed Vasilissa out the door and into the dark night.

Vasilissa sat down and fed her doll a bit of food.

"I am frightened!" she told the doll. "I need your help!"

"Do not worry," the doll replied. "I will protect you."

Baba Yaga lived deep in the forest that bordered the village. Vasilissa stumbled through the dark woods until she came to Baba Yaga's hut. It was perched on chicken legs. Animal skulls hung from the gate, eerily lit with flames. Vasilissa could hear Baba Yaga's hideous cackle inside the hut.

Baba Yaga approached Vasilissa and told her she must work for the light she was seeking. The witch ordered Vasilissa to bring her all of the food from the oven. Baba Yaga ate enough for three people, but she gave Vasilissa only a bit of bread. Vasilissa put it in her pocket.

Baba Yaga told Vasilissa that the next day she would have to scrub the floors, do the washing, cook supper, and clean an entire bushel of wheat while Baba Yaga was away. Otherwise, she would never allow Vasilissa to go home again.

When Baba Yaga fell asleep, Vasilissa took out her doll and told her of the witch's demands.

The doll said, "Go to sleep. You have nothing to fear."

When Vasilissa awoke the next morning, Baba Yaga was already gone. Vasilissa found that all of her tasks had already been done! Vasilissa thanked her doll and rested.

When Baba Yaga returned, she was astounded.

"How did you finish this work?" demanded Baba Yaga.

Vasilissa could not tell her about the doll, but she wished to be truthful.

She said, "My dead mother's blessings helped me."

The witch screamed, "Blessings! We will have no blessings in this house! Be off with you!"

Vasilissa ran as fast as she could. As she passed the fence, she grabbed a glowing skull for light.

When she reached her home, Vasilissa found that her stepmother and stepsisters had fled. They did not want her father to know what they had done to Vasilissa.

The next day, Vasilissa's father returned from his journey. When Vasilissa saw him, she wept tears of joy. Vasilissa and her father lived together happily. She kept her doll and her mother's blessing with her always.

Beauty and the Beast

Adapted by Amy Adair
Illustrated by David Merrell

There once was a rich man who had three daughters. After a lifetime of prosperity, he fell upon hard times when the ships with which he made his living were lost at sea.

His family was forced to move into a small cottage, which made his two elder daughters very unhappy. But the man's youngest daughter, Beauty, remained hopeful.

One day, he received word that one of his lost ships had sailed safely into harbor. He decided to make the difficult journey to the port to see the ship for himself.

It was winter, and he traveled by horseback. His trip was slow and very cold.

Worst of all, when he reached the port, he learned that his ship had been robbed. Now he was even poorer than before.

In sadness, he began the long journey home. It was very cold in the forest, and it began to snow. The man could barely see the trail before him.

Suddenly, he spotted green trees and a lush garden in the distance! To his astonishment, he saw a castle rising ahead of him like a dream.

He had stumbled upon an enchanted castle! He saw a row of flowering trees and felt a summery breeze on his face.

The man went a little farther and found himself in the middle of a sunny garden. Instantly, the snow melted off of his coat, and warmth returned to his fingers and toes.

He knocked several times on the castle door. When no one answered, he pushed open the huge door with all of his might and stepped into the echoing hall.

He explored the castle until he found a little room with a tableful of food. He ate his fill and then fell asleep by the fire.

The next morning, as he was leaving the castle through the gardens, the man spotted a rosebush. He stopped and plucked a rose for his daughters. Suddenly, a horrible beast appeared as if by magic!

"Is this how you thank me?" roared the beast. "I feed and shelter you, and then you steal from me?" The man explained that the flower was a gift for his children.

The beast demanded that the man give up one of his beloved daughters to repay the debt.

"Please, beast. Take me, instead!" pleaded the poor man.

But the beast would not change his mind. He did, however, allow the man to return home and tell his children what had happened.

The two elder daughters both refused to go live with the beast.

"I will go," said Beauty quietly. "You have sacrificed so much for us, Father. Please, let me help you."

Beauty's father was very sad because he loved her greatly. But he also knew that she was strong and brave.

The next day, Beauty and her father traveled to the castle, where the beast greeted them. At first Beauty was frightened by his terrible face, but he spoke gently to her.

"Are you willing to stay with me in order to save your father?" he asked.

Beauty looked into the beast's eyes and saw that they were kind. "Yes," she answered, "I will stay."

The next day, after Beauty's father left, she began trying to make the castle her home. The beast had given her a special room. It had mirrored walls and a clock that woke her by calling out her name.

As time went on, Beauty began to feel happier in the castle. She spent her days exploring its wonderful rooms, corridors, and staircases. Every evening she dined with the beast. Then Beauty and the beast would stroll together through the enchanted garden.

One day, the beast asked Beauty to marry him.

"Oh, please do not ask me that," she told the beast. "I am happy here with you, but I miss my family terribly. I am afraid that I will never see them again."

Although the beast knew he would miss Beauty, he allowed her to return home for a visit.

He let Beauty fill a trunk with gifts for her family and gave her a special gift—a magic ring. When she turned the ring on her finger, it would take her wherever she wished.

That night, Beauty used the magic ring. The next morning she awoke to the sound of her father's voice. She was home! Her family was delighted to see her.

Later, as Beauty pulled gifts from the trunk, her family marveled at the beast's generosity.

"This is the most beautiful necklace I have ever seen," Beauty's eldest sister said.

Beauty's family made a wonderful feast that night to welcome her home. Everyone gathered around and listened while Beauty described the enchanted castle and the beautiful gardens. She also told them how much she had grown to care for her friend the beast.

Beauty enjoyed the time she spent with her family. But as the days passed, she began to miss the beast.

One night, Beauty took the magic ring out of her jewelry box and placed it on her finger. When she looked deep into the jewel, she saw the beast lying in his garden. He looked like he was very ill.

"Oh, my poor beast!" cried Beauty. With that, she turned the ring on her finger and was magically returned to the garden.

Beauty found the beast lying on the ground and rushed to his side. When she lifted his head, he opened his eyes. He wanted to look at her one last time.

"Please don't leave me!" cried Beauty. "I love you!"

The beast's eyes lit up when he heard Beauty say those wonderful words.

Suddenly, there was a flash of light, and the beast was transformed into a handsome prince!

"Thank you!" exclaimed the prince. "Many years ago, I was placed under a spell by an evil enchantress. Only true love could have released me from it," he explained as he took Beauty's hand.

"Will you marry me, Beauty?" the prince whispered.

"Yes," answered Beauty.

Beauty and the prince lived happily ever after.

Rumpelstiltskin

Adapted by Maureen DuChamp
Illustrated by David Hohn

There once lived a poor miller who had nothing but his mill and his good daughter. More than anything, he wanted to give his daughter a happy and comfortable life.

One day, the miller had a chance to meet the king. Hoping to capture the king's attention, the miller boasted of his extraordinary daughter. He spoke of her intelligence, kindness, and beauty. He even claimed that the girl could spin ordinary straw into gold!

The king was intrigued. The next day, he asked the miller's daughter to come to the palace. He showed her to a room filled only with straw and a spinning wheel, and asked her to spin it all into gold by the next morning.

The young woman had no idea how to spin gold from straw. At a loss for what to do, she began to cry.

Suddenly, a little man appeared from out of nowhere. "Why are you crying?" he asked.

The young woman explained.

"I can spin this straw into gold for you," he said. "But you must give me your necklace in return."

The miller's daughter agreed, and she handed him her necklace. It was the only thing of value that she owned, but she did not know what else to do.

The little man set to work. Soon, the young woman fell asleep. When she awoke, the room was full of golden thread. The king was very pleased.

"This is a most remarkable talent you have," he said. "If you can repeat what you have done by tomorrow morning, I will make you my queen."

He showed her into another room, filled with even more straw. No sooner had the door closed than she began to cry.

Once again, the little man appeared.

"I will help you spin this straw into gold," he said. "But this time I will require something of greater value. You must promise me your firstborn child."

The woman hesitated. How could she make such a promise? But in her desperation, she agreed.

The odd little man set to work, and the young woman fell asleep. She awoke to find the straw spun into gold.

When the king arrived, he was amazed.

"Will you be my bride?" he asked.

"Yes," said the young woman, "on one condition. You must promise never to ask me to spin straw into gold again."

The king agreed. And soon he and the miller's daughter were wed.

Though at first the new queen thought that her husband was a bit greedy, she soon found him to be a sweet and caring man and a noble king. They grew to love each other very much.

Within a year of their wedding, their first child was born.

The queen was so happy that she forgot all about her promise to the little man who had helped her. It was not until he appeared at her window one day that she remembered.

"Your Highness," said the odd man, "I have come to claim what is mine—your firstborn child. Your son belongs to me."

"Surely you will not take my child," said the queen. "I was a fool to make such a promise. Now that I am queen, I can give you anything you desire."

"What I desire," he answered, "is your child. You must keep your promise to me."

The little man squinted his eyes. He considered the queen as she cradled her child in her arms. Finally, he sighed.

"I can see how much you care for your son," he said. "Therefore, I will give you a chance to keep him. If you can guess my name, I will forgive your promise."

"Horace?" the queen asked quickly. "Is your name Hubert? Hal? Henry?"

"Ha," he bellowed. "It is none of those. I will give you two more chances to guess."

With that, he turned and left the castle. The queen ordered one of her porters to follow him. The servant secretly watched the little man as he traveled deep into the forest. He set up camp, built a fire, and danced happily around it. He knew the queen would never guess his name.

Meanwhile, the queen compiled a list. She sent for her royal advisers and asked them for the most unusual names they could find. They scoured the countryside and reported their findings to the queen.

The next day, the queen's porter returned to the castle. He had very little to report. The little man had danced around his fire all night long, but he did not speak a word.

Suddenly, a voice startled the queen.

"Have you any guesses for me, Your Highness?" asked the little man. He had appeared from out of nowhere.

"Indeed, I do," she said. "Are you called Monty? Mal? Montivecchio? Well, then Orton? Opyrus? Orenthal? Or perhaps you are Balthazar? Bitmillymont? Bugleheim?"

The queen read every name from her list.

"All of your guesses are wrong!" said the little man triumphantly. "I will give you one more chance."

The queen returned to her list of names. She again asked her porter to follow the little man.

The porter found the little man in the same spot, deep in the forest. And just as he had the night before, the man began to dance around his fire. This time, however, he sang a little song as he danced.

The queen's heart will surely break,
For tomorrow her child I'll take.
But now we play a guessing game,
And Rumpelstiltskin is my name!

The queen's porter smiled as he heard the mysterious name revealed. He made the long journey back to the palace, arriving only moments before the little man.

"It is time for your final guesses," said the little man.

"You do not look like an Alphonso or a Louie," said the queen. "You must be a Rumpelstiltskin."

"That is impossible!" cried the man. "How could you know?"

In his fury, Rumpelstiltskin's face turned red. He stomped his foot so hard on the floor that a hole opened up beneath him. Rumpelstiltskin disappeared into the hole and was never heard from again.

In the end, the king and queen, the handsome little prince, and the miller lived happily ever after.

Three Little Pigs

Adapted by Austin Burley
Illustrated by Susan Spellman

One day, a mother pig told her three little pigs that it was time for them to go out into the world to make their own way.

The three brothers gave their mother a farewell kiss and set out. They followed the path into the countryside. While they walked, they enjoyed the warm sunshine on their heads and the fresh, clean smell of the grass in the meadow.

As the sun reached its highest point in the sky, the three pigs came across a man who was selling straw. The first little pig felt that straw would be a fine material with which to build his house. He bought all the straw the man had and soon built himself a lovely little cottage on the edge of the meadow.

Just as the first little pig was settling into his comfortable straw chair, there came a knock on his door. It was a wolf!

"Little pig! Little pig! Let me in!" said the wolf.

"Not by the hair on my chinny-chin-chin!" squealed the pig from inside his new straw home.

"Then I'll huff, and I'll puff, and I'll blow your house down!" said the big, bad wolf.

The wolf huffed, and he puffed, and he blew the house down. The first little pig scampered quickly away.

The second little pig had met a man carrying a bundle of sticks. The pig bought the sticks and built himself a lovely little cottage.

It was not long after he finished that the big, bad wolf came along. He knocked loudly on the door, saying, "Little pig! Little pig! Let me in!"

"Not by the hair on my chinny-chin-chin!" said the second little pig.

"Then I'll huff, and I'll puff, and I'll blow your house down!" threatened the wolf.

The wolf huffed, and he puffed, and he blew the house down. The second little pig ran away as fast as he could.

The third little pig had happened to meet a man carrying a load of bricks. This pig bought the man's bricks and built himself a very snug and sturdy little cottage near his brothers.

It did not take long for the wolf to find the third pig. "Little pig! Little pig! Let me in!" growled the wolf.

"Not by the hair on my chinny-chin-chin!" squealed the third little pig.

"Then I'll huff, and I'll puff, and I'll blow your house down!" roared the wolf.

The wolf huffed, and he puffed. Then he puffed, and he huffed. But he could not blow the little house down. The bricks were just too strong.

"Hmmm," said the wolf. And he quickly made a new plan.

"Little pig," he said, "Mr. Monroe's farm has a nice field of turnips. If you would like, I could take you there at six o'clock tomorrow morning."

The little pig agreed. But he was too smart for the wolf. He awoke at five o'clock, went to the field, got the turnips, and was back in his house when the wolf arrived at six.

The wolf was very angry that he had been tricked. He thought of a new plan.

"Little pig," he said sweetly, "there is a tree full of juicy apples, just up the road in Granny Smith's garden. I will show you at five o'clock tomorrow morning."

The little pig woke up at four o'clock and hurried off to find the apples. The wolf also awoke at four o'clock and went to the garden to wait for the little pig.

Just as the wolf thought, the little pig was already carrying some juicy red apples down from the tree when he arrived.

The little pig was frightened. The wolf came close and called up to him.

"My, you are up early," said the wolf. "How are the apples?"

"Delicious!" answered the pig. "Why don't you stand back? I will throw one down to you."

The little pig tossed the apple as far as he could. He threw it so far that he was able to scoot down the tree and run away. The little pig was safely home before the wolf found the apple he had thrown.

Back at his little brick house, the pig made applesauce and apple pie, and he still had plenty of apples left to eat.

Not being one to give up, the wolf went back to the little pig's house the very next day.

"Little pig," said the wolf, "there is a fair in town today. Let us go together! I will come by for you at three this afternoon."

The pig agreed. But, of course, he went much earlier. He wanted to be home before the wolf came.

The little pig was on his way home with a barrel he had won at the fair, when he saw the wolf approaching.

The smart little pig crawled into the barrel. He rocked it back and forth until it tipped over and began to roll down the hill. The barrel with the little pig inside headed straight for the wolf! This frightened the wolf so much that he ran right home.

The next day, the wolf knocked on the little pig's door.

"Little pig," he said, "I was on my way to meet you at the fair yesterday, when the most frightening thing came rolling down the hill at me. I ran straight home!"

The little pig laughed. "I am afraid it was I that frightened you! I was in the barrel!"

The wolf was very unhappy to hear this.

"Little pig," roared the wolf, "I am going to eat you for dinner today! I could not blow your house down, and I could not trick you. But now I will certainly come down the chimney to get you!"

The little pig had hung a pot filled with water over the fire. The wolf tumbled down the chimney, right into the boiling water! The pig quickly put a heavy lid on the pot. And that was the end of the big, bad wolf.

Later that evening, there was a knock on the little pig's door. He was relieved to find his two brothers standing there. The three of them enjoyed turnip salad, apple pie, and a barrelful of applesauce as they lived happily ever after.

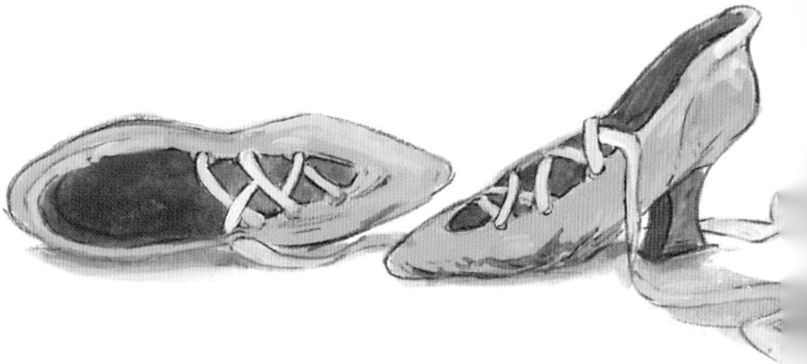

Twelve Dancing Princesses

Adapted by Michael P. Fertig
Illustrated by Jeffrey Ebbeler

Once upon a time in a faraway kingdom, there lived a king with twelve daughters. To say that having twelve daughters was a handful would be unfair to the king, for it was far more than that. The king was a very protective father, and he worried about his little princesses. Also, he did not always understand their ways. This was especially true since the death of his dear wife some years ago.

Each night, the king carefully locked the door to his daughters' bedroom. Yet, each morning, he found the princesses tired and out of sorts. More puzzling still, every morning he found their new pairs of silk dancing slippers worn to shreds.

When the king asked his daughters about this, they would laugh and say, "Don't be silly, Father. We go to sleep each night and sleep soundly until the morning."

But the king was not convinced. He decided to offer a reward to any man from his kingdom who could solve this mystery.

The next day, one of the king's subjects—a man called Rawling—was out walking in the countryside. He was a poor but clever man, and he liked to walk and think. He had just stopped to eat his modest lunch when a strange little woman came hobbling by.

"Good day," said Rawling, standing to greet her. "Would you care for some lunch?"

"Thank you," said the old woman. "You are very kind to share with me when you have so little." In return, she gave him a cloak that could make him invisible. "Take it to the castle," she said, "and claim the king's reward."

Thanking the old woman, Rawling set off for the castle. When he arrived, the king was eager to see if this young man would succeed in solving the mystery. Several others had already tried and failed.

When Rawling met the princesses, they offered him a goblet of wine.

"Thank you," said Rawling. But he was suspicious that it contained a sleeping draft. When the princesses turned away, Rawling poured it beneath the table.

Rawling pretended to yawn. He was then shown to his bed, where he pretended to fall asleep.

"It is safe now," said the eldest princess. "He will sleep until morning, like all the others."

With that, she tapped three times on a bedpost. The bed rose from the floor, revealing a secret staircase. The princesses ran down the winding stairs.

Rawling, wearing his cloak, followed. He stepped upon the youngest princess's gown. She was startled but could see no one when she turned around.

At the bottom of the stairs was an enchanted forest. The trees had branches of gold and silver and diamonds.

Twelve princes met the princesses and guided them to gondolas. Then they rowed across a lake to a beautiful castle. Rawling stole onto one of the boats. The prince who rowed thought the boat seemed heavier than usual.

The twelve princesses and the twelve princes walked arm in arm into a grand ballroom within the castle. Rawling crept softly behind them, marveling at all that he found there.

Beautiful music seemed to float from the ceiling. Clusters of candles hung in the air, casting a soft glow. The wonderful room was enchanted.

The princesses and princes began to dance splendidly around the ballroom. Each pair moved more gracefully than the next, and their movements were perfectly in step with the joyful music. Rawling watched, enthralled.

The couples danced for hours, only pausing to sip punch from golden goblets. Then, finally, the princes escorted the twelve princesses back to the secret staircase.

Fortunately, the twelve princesses were tired from their evening of dancing so they walked slowly. Rawling was able to hurry ahead of them and slip back into his bed before they returned.

The youngest princess peeked in on him.

"Our handsome guest is sleeping as though he's lived a thousand lives," she told her sisters. With that, the princesses removed their tattered dancing slippers and placed them in a row. Then they climbed into their own beds and fell asleep.

The next morning, Rawling crept out of bed and went to find the king. He carried with him proof of all he had seen the night before, following the princesses.

"Your Majesty," said Rawling, "I have solved your riddle. It seems that your lovely daughters wear out their slippers by dancing late at night." And he told the king all he knew.

The king listened intently. "Can you produce proof of this story?" he asked.

Rawling presented a golden goblet.

"This, Your Majesty, is a goblet from the castle," Rawling said. "I ask you to put your lips to it."

The king raised the goblet to his lips, and it instantly filled with punch.

"How is this possible?" asked the king.

"The goblet is enchanted," said Rawling.

Rawling then laid out three tree branches. One had leaves of gold, one had leaves of silver, and the last had leaves of diamonds.

"These are from the forest near the castle," Rawling explained. "But the greatest proof of my tale must come from your own daughters."

The princesses, who were listening at the door, confirmed what Rawling had said.

The king was pleased. "You have solved this great mystery," he said. "I owe you a great reward."

"Your Majesty," spoke Rawling, "in my brief time with your daughters, I have grown fond of your youngest." Rawling looked at the princess. "If she will agree, I should like to ask for her hand in marriage."

The young princess smiled. She had been charmed by the brave and clever man. The king granted Rawling's request, and the princess agreed to marry him.

The pair lived—and danced—happily ever after.

The Little Dutch Boy

Adapted by Sarah Toast
Illustrated by Linda Dockey Graves

Long ago there was a boy named Hans. He lived with his mother in a pretty little town in Holland. As you may know, the land in Holland is very flat and also lower than the sea. Dutch farmers have built high walls, called dikes, to keep the sea from flooding their farms.

Like all Dutch children, little Hans knew that if a dike were to break, the fields would fill with seawater. The town would then be ruined.

One day, Hans's mother packed a lunch basket for him to take to their friend, Mr. Van Notten. He lived outside of town, and it was a very long walk to his house.

Before Hans left, his mother reminded him to leave Mr. Van Notten's house in plenty of time to walk home before it grew dark.

On his way out of town, Hans followed the road that ran along the dike. After a time, he arrived at Mr. Van Notten's house.

Mr. Van Notten lived alone, and he was always glad when Hans would come for a visit.

Hans was quite hungry after his long walk, so Mr. Van Notten made cocoa and set out the bread and cheese that Hans's mother had sent. After their meal, the boy and the old man talked by the fire.

When Mr. Van Notten's dog scratched at the door to be let outside, Hans noticed that the sky had become dark and stormy. He knew he should leave before it began to rain.

Although the boy walked quickly, he was not halfway home when the wind began to gust. A cold rain fell on Hans as he struggled against the wind. The weather made walking very difficult.

"Put one foot in front of the other," he told himself. "You will be home soon."

The strong wind made the trees bend low, and it flattened the flowers to the ground. Hans was quite cold by now, and he had to hold on to his hat to keep it from blowing away.

"I hope mother won't be upset when I arrive home so cold and wet and muddy," he thought.

Hans kept his head down against the wind as he trudged along the road. It was so dark that Hans did not know where he was until he lifted his head and saw the dike in front of him. This meant that he would be home very soon.

Even through the raindrops, Hans noticed that something was wrong with the dike. He could see a small hole in the wall allowing a trickle of water to seep through.

Hans knew immediately what must have happened. The storm had whipped up big waves in the sea on the other side of the dike. The pounding water had caused the wall to crack.

Hans knew he had to warn everyone in town that the dike had sprung a leak. They were in great danger.

He ran into town yelling, "The dike is breaking! Help! We must repair the dike!"

But no one heard him.

All of the townspeople were snug in their homes. Every house and store in town was shut up tight against the storm. The doors were bolted, and the windows were shuttered to protect against the wind and rain.

Hans realized that no one could hear his cries. He stopped running, caught his breath, and considered what to do. He knew his mother must be worried about him, but the hole in the dike was growing every minute.

Hans knew that if the hole got too big, the sea would break through and wash away the town.

As fast as he could, Hans ran back to the place where he had seen the water seeping through the dike. Just as he thought, the crack had grown bigger.

Hans knew that the crack must be fixed right away. He could think of nothing else to do, so Hans balled up his fist and pushed it into the hole to stop the seawater from pouring through.

Hans felt proud as he stood there, holding back the sea. He was sure that his mother would send people to look for him. But minutes turned into hours as Hans stood there, patiently protecting the dike.

As darkness fell, Hans was very cold and tired. His arm had begun to ache, and he had to force himself to remain standing.

He thought about the warmth of the fireplace at home as he stood in the cold rain by the dike. Then he thought about how good it would feel to lie down in his own little bed.

When Hans did not come home that evening, his mother began to worry. As the rain fell, she kept watch, hoping Hans would return. Eventually, she decided that Hans must have stayed at Mr. Van Notten's house while he waited for the storm to pass.

Early the next morning, Mr. Van Notten walked to Hans's home. He wanted to thank Hans for his visit yesterday and thank his mother for the tasty food.

When he came upon Hans, the brave little boy was trembling with cold. Hans's arm hurt from the effort of keeping his fist wedged in the hole, and his legs were ready to collapse from standing all night. Still, Hans had to hold firm for just a little longer while Mr. Van Notten ran into town to alert the townspeople and find some help.

"Don't worry, Hans," said Mr. Van Notten. "I will be back as soon as I can. You are doing fine. Just hang on a little longer."

Soon Mr. Van Notten returned with help. The townspeople began working to repair the dike as Mr. Van Notten wrapped Hans in blankets and carried him home to his mother. She put Hans to bed and gave him some warm broth to drink. Then she rubbed his fingers and his stiff legs to warm them up.

Word quickly spread through the town about how brave Hans had held back the sea all by himself. The townspeople were very curious. They went to the dike to see the hole that Hans had plugged.

As soon as Hans was warm and felt strong enough, he and his mother took a trip to the dike to see the repairs that were being made.

Everyone was overjoyed to see Hans. They gave him gifts fit for a hero. They shook his hand and marveled that he had been able to hold back the sea all by himself. Over and over, they thanked the boy for saving them from a terrible flood.

Hans was very proud. He never imagined that he might one day save his town. His mother smiled down at him. She was very proud, too.

The town's mayor held a beautiful ceremony for Hans. He presented the boy with a medal in honor of the strength and courage he had shown in the face of grave danger. Everyone cheered loudly. They were also proud of young Hans.

Years later, after Hans had grown into a man, people continued to call him the little boy with the big heart. To this day, he has not been forgotten.

The Wild Swans

Adapted by Lara Ehrlich
Illustrated by Kathy Mitchell

Once upon a time in a faraway land, there lived a good king and his four children. His wife had died, leaving him to raise three sons and a daughter on his own. The queen had been a beautiful and gentle woman who had spent her days in the garden among her rosebushes.

The king's youngest child, Rosalind, reminded him of the queen. From the time she was small, Rosalind loved to tend her mother's roses. As she grew, Rosalind was as good and kind a daughter as any man could wish for.

The king's three brave sons spent their hours as most princes do, hunting in the forest. One day, they caught sight of a white stag at the edge of the clearing.

They chased the stag through the forest from dawn until dusk, but it slipped soundlessly through the brush. As night fell, the princes followed the stag into the kingdom of Queen Maeve, the ruler of the fairies. Queen Maeve heard the princes crashing through her trees and, in a rage, turned them into wild swans.

Wailing mournfully, the swan princes flew over the castle walls and disappeared into the night sky. Rosalind heard their cries and opened her window. She saw her beloved brothers rise in front of the moon and disappear.

The king fell into a deep sadness. Even Rosalind, who had always made her father so happy, could do nothing for him. So Rosalind took leave of her father and set out in search of her brothers. She traveled far and wide, until one evening she came to an ocean. On the shore, Rosalind found three white feathers.

As she bent to gather the feathers, an old woman wandered down the shore carrying a heavy basket. Rosalind took the old woman's basket upon her own back and helped her cross the rocky beach.

"Thank you, my dear," the old woman said, smiling kindly. "What are you doing here all alone?"

Rosalind clutched the three feathers to her breast and replied, "I am searching for my brothers who have been transformed into swans. Have you seen any swans nearby?"

The old woman nodded thoughtfully and pointed toward a rocky cove in the distance. Rosalind turned her head to look. When she turned back again, the old woman had vanished.

Rosalind hid in the brush to wait and see if the swans would appear. Finally, as the sun began to set, three swans flew over the ocean and came to rest in the cove.

Although she longed to call out to them, Rosalind held her breath for fear that she would frighten the swans away. As the last of the sun's rays disappeared over the horizon, a startling change occurred. The swans lifted their long necks and transformed into men. Rosalind could wait no longer and ran onto the beach, into her brothers' arms.

"We have only until sunrise," the princes told her. "Then we will become swans once again, and we must fly back over the ocean."

"Then I will go with you," Rosalind replied.

The princes worked all night making a net to carry their sister. At dawn, when they again became swans, they carried her over the ocean to their cave.

While her brothers hunted for food, Rosalind curled up on a pile of leaves and fell into a restless sleep. She dreamed of the old woman she had met on the beach.

In Rosalind's dream, the old woman transformed into a beautiful and frightening queen.

"I am Queen Maeve," the queen told her. "Because of your kindness to me, I will give you one chance to save your brothers. But it will require great sacrifice from you."

Queen Maeve swept her arm across the cave, and rosebushes appeared all around her.

"From these roses, you must craft three shirts, one for each brother. When you cover the swans with them, the spell will be broken. But you may not speak until the shirts have been completed. If you do, your words will pierce your brothers' hearts like arrows."

Rosalind awoke to find the cave filled with rosebushes. When her brothers returned, she was sewing the rose petals into a fine cloth. Although she could not explain, her brothers knew that she was helping them.

The swan princes brought Rosalind food and water and kept her warm in the shelter of their wings. She worked for many days and nights, barely pausing to rest.

One evening, a woodcutter and his wife discovered the cave as they were walking along the shore. The woodcutter's wife had never seen such lovely roses, and she stepped inside the cave for a closer look.

There, among the roses, she found Rosalind sewing petals into cloth. The couple took pity on the young girl alone in the cave. They insisted she return with them to their cottage, and Rosalind could not speak to resist.

As they left the cave, Rosalind gathered as many roses as she could carry. She stayed with the couple for many days and did all that they asked of her. But Rosalind did not forget the dear brothers. She spent every moment she could spare sewing their garments from rose petals.

When two shirts were complete and the third lacked only a sleeve, Rosalind sewed the last petal from her final rose. What could she do? She had to finish her task.

The woodcutter's wife had a rosebush that she loved above all else. Rosalind wept as she crept outside into the dark and plucked the petals from the beloved flowers. She sewed through the night, and at sunrise, she had finished the last shirt.

"You have stolen my roses!" cried the woodcutter's wife when she saw what Rosalind had done.

Rosalind fled from the house with the shirts. She raced toward her brothers, calling to them as she ran. When they heard her cries, they flew down from the sky. Rosalind quickly threw the shirts over them. The instant she did so, the three swans were transformed into three handsome princes.

Now that the spell was broken, Rosalind returned to the cottage to tell her story to the woodcutter and his wife.

"I am sorry to have hurt you when you were so kind to me," she said. "My brothers and I will repay you."

When all was forgiven, Rosalind and her brothers began their long journey home.

The good king had all but given up hope of seeing his children again. When Rosalind and her brothers returned, the king was certain that his eyes deceived him. Only when his children flocked around him and swept into his arms could he believe it was true. The kingdom commenced a celebration that lasted for many months.

The princes were careful never to hunt in Queen Maeve's forest again, and Rosalind returned to her rose garden. She sent her loveliest rose bush to the woodcutter's wife, and the roses bloomed all year round.

Snow White and the Seven Dwarves

Adapted by Lara Ehrlich
Illustrated by Barbara Lanza

Once upon a time in a peaceful kingdom by the sea, the king and queen were blessed with a baby girl. Her hair was black as night, her lips were red as rubies, and her skin was white as snow. The queen named her Snow White.

There was great rejoicing throughout the kingdom. But the joy soon turned to mourning when the queen fell ill and died.

After many months, the king remarried. However, the woman he chose as his bride was very different from Snow White's mother.

The new queen was wicked and vain. She cared for nothing but her own beauty.

Every morning, the queen would visit her magic mirror and ask the same question: "Mirror, mirror, on the wall, who in this realm is the fairest of all?"

Every morning, the magic mirror replied, "You, my queen, are the fairest of all."

For years, the mirror gave the same answer to the queen's question. The queen gave no thought to Snow White, who was growing into a beautiful young woman. Beloved by everyone in the kingdom, Snow White was as gentle and kind as she was lovely.

One day, the queen visited the mirror and asked the usual question. This time she received a different answer. "You, my queen, may have a beauty quite rare, but Snow White is a thousand times more fair."

Mad with jealousy, the queen sent for the royal huntsman.

She ordered him to take Snow White into the forest and kill her at once. Fearing for his life, the huntsman took Snow White into the woods. When she looked up at him with her gentle eyes, full of trust, the huntsman could not bring himself to carry out the queen's order. He left Snow White in the forest and warned her never to return to the castle.

The sky grew dark as Snow White wandered deeper and deeper into the forest. Her dress caught on the brush, and she heard a wolf howl in the distance. Snow White was terribly frightened, but she willed herself to continue walking.

Just when Snow White feared she could not take another step, she found herself in a clearing beside a tiny cottage. She knocked once on the wooden door, but there was no answer. The force of her knock caused the door to swing open, and Snow White stepped inside.

She saw seven little cups and seven little plates on a table surrounded by seven little chairs. Seven little nightshirts hung on seven little hooks, and along one wall stood seven little beds. The cottage was cozy but untidy.

"Perhaps if I tidy this little cottage," she thought, "no one would mind if I have a bit of dinner and warm myself by the fire."

Snow White cleaned the cottage until it shone. Only then did she take a bit of bread. She sat down on one of the beds to wait for someone to come home.

Snow White was so tired, and the bed was so cozy, that she soon fell fast asleep.

While she slept, seven dwarves came into the clearing. They sang and talked as they opened the door, but fell silent at the sight of the maiden sleeping on the bed. She looked so peaceful that they let her sleep.

Snow White awoke to find herself surrounded by seven kind faces. The dwarves welcomed her to the cottage and asked how she had found their home. Snow White told the dwarves about the evil queen and her flight through the dark forest.

The dwarves took pity on Snow White and asked her to stay with them. She was happy to keep the house tidy and make supper for the dwarves.

Back at the castle, the evil queen gazed into her mirror and asked, "Mirror, mirror, on the wall, who in this realm is the fairest of all?"

The mirror replied, "You, my queen, have a beauty quite rare, but beyond the mountains, where the seven dwarves dwell, Snow White is thriving, and this I must tell: Within this realm she's still a thousand times more fair."

The queen flew into a rage. She began to search for Snow White. When the queen found the cottage in the clearing, she disguised herself as a poor seamstress, calling out, "Gowns for sale!"

Snow White welcomed the seamstress and tried on one of the lovely dresses. The evil queen pulled the laces so tight that Snow White could not breathe, and she fell to the floor, bound in the lovely gown.

The dwarves came home that evening to find Snow White lying motionless on the ground. They quickly cut the laces that stifled her and, to their great relief, she breathed deeply and opened her eyes.

That night the queen triumphantly asked her mirror, "Mirror, mirror, on the wall, who in this realm is the fairest of all?" And again, the mirror replied with the same answer: Snow White was fairer than the queen.

White with rage, the queen filled the teeth of her prettiest comb with deadly poison. The next morning, she disguised herself as a peddler and set out through the woods to the little cottage.

Snow White welcomed the peddler into the cottage and admired the silver combs. The queen selected the most beautiful one and gently brushed Snow White's long, black hair.

The moment the comb touched her head, Snow White fell to the ground and her hair tangled around her, black as night.

When the dwarves returned home, they found Snow White on the floor. As the sad dwarves carried Snow White to her bed, the comb fell from her hair.

She opened her eyes and smiled up at them. The dwarves rejoiced, but they were worried that the queen would try to harm Snow White again. They made Snow White promise not to open the door for anyone but themselves.

The queen returned to the mirror and gazed proudly at her reflection. "Mirror, mirror, on the wall, who in this realm is the fairest of all?" Again, the mirror answered that Snow White was a thousand times more fair than the queen.

Shaking with fury, the queen thought for a very long time. Finally, she had an idea she was certain would not fail. The queen plucked the finest apple from the orchard and poisoned the shiniest half. She disguised herself as a poor farmer woman and set off through the woods, carrying a basket of apples on her arm.

"Apples for sale!" the queen called out from the yard. This time, Snow White heeded the seven dwarves and did not open the door.

Snow White spoke to the farmer woman from the window. "Thank you, good woman," she said, "but I have no need for apples today."

The queen replied, "These are not just any apples." She held the poisoned apple up to the window and said, "These are the reddest and ripest apples in the kingdom. There is nothing to fear—I shall show you."

The queen cut the apple in half, and ate the unpoisoned half herself.

She offered the other half through the window to Snow White. Snow White thanked her kindly, certain that such a lovely apple posed no threat. She took one bite and fell lifeless to the ground, her skin as pale as snow. The queen smiled and slipped off into the woods, filled with satisfaction.

This time when the dwarves returned home, they could do nothing to wake Snow White. She looked as pretty and peaceful as if she were sleeping. The dwarves wept for a very long time, then they placed Snow White in a glass case so they could watch over her while they worked.

One day, a handsome prince rode through the forest and saw Snow White sleeping. Startled, he asked the dwarves, "Who is this beautiful lady? How did she come to be here?"

The dwarves told him about Snow White and the wicked queen, and how they could do nothing to awaken her. The prince replied, "I will take her to my castle until she awakens. Then, if she is willing, I will ask her to be my wife."

He hitched the glass case to his horse, and the dwarves accompanied him on the way to his castle. As they rode through the forest, the case jostled and the bit of poisoned apple fell from Snow White's mouth. Her eyes fluttered open, and she smiled up at the prince.

The wedding celebration lasted for many days, and there was great rejoicing throughout the kingdom.

There were dances and feasts, and Snow White was happier than she had ever been. While the kingdom celebrated, the evil queen crept into the forest and was never seen again. Snow White and her prince ruled the kingdom with kindness and wisdom and lived happily ever after.

The Frog Prince

Adapted by Michael P. Fertig
Illustrated by Kathy Mitchell

Once upon a time in a kingdom far away, there lived a king who had many beautiful children. The king's youngest daughter, Princess Annabel, was the most playful of the family.

Princess Annabel loved to explore the many lovely gardens that surrounded the castle. Her favorite toy was a golden ball that her father had given to her. Again and again, she would toss the ball into the air, catching it as it fell back down. It was a game she was quite good at—until the day she threw the ball too high. It bounced wildly off of a tree branch and fell into the well in the center of the garden.

Annabel ran to the edge of the well. It was much too deep for her to climb into. She began to cry softly. She loved her golden ball.

"Please, don't cry," said a little voice.

"Who's there?" asked Annabel. She looked around, but no one else was in the garden. There was only a little frog looking up at her. "You did not speak just now, did you?" she said to the frog.

"Well, of course I did," said the frog. "I hate to see princesses cry. I will swim to the bottom of the well and find your ball. But you must do something for me."

"Yes, anything," said Annabel. "Would you like a kiss?"

"A kiss?" said the frog with a grimace. "No, thank you. All I want is for you to invite me to dinner tonight with you and your family."

"Certainly," said Princess Annabel.

The little frog dove right into the well and swam to the bottom. He easily found the golden ball and swam back to the surface with it.

"Oh, thank you," said Annabel. "Now, please join my family and me for dinner."

Annabel scooped up the frog and headed back to the castle, just as dinner was being laid on the table.

"What is this frog doing here?" asked the king.

Annabel quickly explained her agreement with the kind frog.

"Very well," said the king. "If you made a promise, then you must keep your word."

No sooner had the first serving platter been placed on the table than the frog began to eat with messy delight. The family watched in amazement as the frog slurped and drooled all over the royal tablecloth.

The little frog ate enough to feed an army of frogs. He ate bread rolls and tossed salad, honey ham and butter-browned turkey, wild potatoes, and four bowls of royal corn chowder.

Princess Annabel was embarrassed that her dinner guest made such a mess at the table. Clearly, this little frog did not have proper manners.

"I hope you have left some room for dessert," she said. After the kindness the frog had shown her, she wanted to be sure he enjoyed his meal. "Here, little frog, you have the first piece of cake."

The frog looked up at her with wide eyes and a big smile. He ate his piece of cake in three bites.

Suddenly, a strange rumbling came from the frog's tummy. Princess Annabel and her father watched in disbelief as the little frog turned into a boy! A prince!

The king stood and looked down at the boy. He could not believe his eyes!

Annabel was in shock. She did not know what to think. "What is happening, Father?" she asked.

"I can explain," said the prince. "My name is Prince Henry. Many years ago, an evil witch cast a spell on me, making me a frog for all eternity. The only way the spell could be broken was for a princess to offer me a piece of cake from her dinner table. I never imagined it could be broken. I am forever grateful for this meal."

"But you are so young," said Annabel.

"I was your age when the spell was cast," he said. "Once I became a frog, I never aged. I look the same today as when I was cursed. But I'm afraid I have been a frog for a very long time. My family and friends are gone. Now I have nowhere to go."

The king decided to adopt Prince Henry.

"We have more than enough room for you," said the king. "And all the cake you can eat."

The prince loved his new family. He especially enjoyed playing catch with his new sister, Princess Annabel, and her golden ball. In the end, everyone lived happily ever after.

The Elves and the Shoemaker

Adapted by Sylvia Vanerka
Illustrated by Jon Goodell

Many winters ago, in a small village not far away, there lived a shoemaker and his wife. For many years they earned a good living making shoes for the people of the town.

It was common knowledge among the villagers that the fine shoes bought from the shoemaker's shop were sure to last a score or more. The little shop was always busy, and the villagers were always satisfied with their shoes. All of this changed, however, after one winter storm.

It was the fiercest snowstorm anyone had ever seen. Even after it stopped snowing, the weight of the snow destroyed several houses. And when the spring thaw came, the melted snow flooded every farm for miles around.

SHOES

As a result of the ruined farmland, many people began to move away. As more and more people left the village, the shoemaker and his wife sold fewer and fewer shoes. Soon, they were down to their last piece of leather. It would be enough to make one more pair of shoes. After that, they did not know what they would do.

The shoemaker was about to cut the leather to make the final pair of shoes, but he decided to wait until morning. He set his tools and the piece of leather on his workbench and climbed upstairs to bed.

The next morning, the shoemaker and his wife came down to the workshop to find a surprise. On his bench sat the finest pair of shoes the shoemaker had ever seen. The shoemaker rubbed his eyes in astonishment.

"My dear," he said to his wife, "I don't expect you made these shoes during the night, did you?"

"No," she replied, "I did not."

"Well, I did not either," he said. "Who did?"

Before his wife could even shrug, the bell of their shop door sounded. A customer entered.

"Hello, good sir and madam," said a well-dressed man. "I am visiting from the city and have stepped in a very large mud puddle. My shoes are decidedly ruined. Do you have anything in my size?"

The shoemaker grabbed the mysterious pair of shoes from his workbench. His wife slid them onto the feet of the well-dressed man. They fit perfectly!

"I say," said the man, "this might be the best-looking pair of shoes I have ever worn! They are certainly the most comfortable."

So pleased was he with the shoes that the well-dressed man paid the shoemaker with a full gold coin.

The gold coin was enough for the shoemaker to buy leather for two new pairs of shoes. Once again, he left the leather and his tools on his workbench and climbed upstairs for bed.

The next morning, the shoemaker and his wife came down to the shop to discover that two more pairs of shoes had been made from the leather he left out.

"How could this be?" said the shoemaker to his wife.

Before she could answer, two ladies walked in.

"Good day," one of them said. "My husband came in yesterday and bought the most glorious pair of shoes. My sister and I would like to find something as well."

As luck had it, the two new pairs of shoes fit perfectly.

"Goodness," said the woman, "these are delightful! I'll tell everyone I know to visit your shop."

And she did. Soon, the shoemaker's shop was bustling.

The two women—and their many friends—paid handsomely for their shoes. The shoemaker and his wife were able to buy more and more leather. And night after night, the leather was sewn into fine pairs of shoes.

"We must discover who is helping us," the shoemaker said to his wife one evening. "Let's stay up late and hide to see who is making these shoes."

The shoemaker and his wife sat quietly in the shadows of their shop. Just after midnight, they heard a sound. They peered around a corner to spy two tiny elves happily at work on a new pair of shoes.

"Why, it's elves!" said the shoemaker's wife. "But look at their clothes. They work so hard to make such fine shoes for us, yet they wear only rags themselves."

The shoemaker's wife decided that the next night she would leave out new suits of clothes to thank the elves.

The next day was another busy one in the shop. The shoemaker and his wife had enough shoes to fill every shelf. At the end of the day, the shoemaker's wife sat down at the workbench. Rather than leaving out pieces of leather, this time she left out two tiny outfits she had sewn herself. She hoped the elves would like them.

The shoemaker and his wife hid once again. Like the night before, they heard a sound just after midnight. When they peered around the corner this time, however, they saw the two tiny elves wearing their new clothes and dancing happily together.

After that night, the elves never returned. But the town was thriving again, due in part to the success of the shoemaker's shop. People traveled for miles to buy shoes there. Times were good again. They all lived happily ever after, thanks to the kindness of two tiny strangers.

The Goose Girl

Adapted by Lisa Harkrader
Illustrated by Cindy Salans Rosenheim

Once there was a princess who was betrothed to a prince whom she had never met. He lived in a distant kingdom. When it was time for the princess to join him there, her mother, a kind and generous queen, gathered clothes and jewels, linens and ornaments, to supply her daughter with everything necessary for her new home.

The queen gave her daughter one last gift.

"This is my royal ring," said the queen. "When you arrive at your new castle, this ring will prove who you are."

The princess slipped the ring onto her finger and joined her companions for the journey. These included a lady-in-waiting from the castle, and her beloved horse Falada, who had the gift of speech.

The little group set off. After a time, the princess grew thirsty, so they stopped by a stream. The princess knelt daintily on the bank and drank from her cupped hands.

As she dipped her hands into the water, her mother's ring slid from her finger. The princess did not notice, but the lady-in-waiting did. The maid waded into the stream and plucked the ring from the current.

"Dear princess," said the lady-in-waiting, "look what I found in the stream." She held out the royal ring.

"Oh, dear!" cried the princess. "You have saved me."

"Yes, I have," said the maid. "Perhaps I should keep this ring for you. And look how you've muddied your gown. You should allow me to take charge of all your belongings. I will ride Falada and keep them safe for you."

"You are very good to me," said the princess. And she switched her clothes and her horse with the maid.

When the travelers reached the castle, the king and the prince were waiting.

"Show me to my room," the lady-in-waiting demanded haughtily. "I am very tired and hungry."

The king was surprised by the young lady's rudeness. But he said politely, "We are delighted that you have arrived safely, Princess."

Then he turned to the real princess, assuming that she was the servant. "We will also find room for you. We understand you are to be our new goose girl. Welcome."

"Thank you," she replied. "But I am the princess."

The lady-in-waiting laughed. "You? Your clothes are mere rags." The maid extended her hand to display the queen's ring. "This ring proves that I am the princess."

The king sent the astonished princess off with the goose boy, Conrad. She did not know what to do!

Each morning, the princess and Conrad led the geese to the meadow. Each night, she slept on straw in the barn.

One day, the princess found Falada in a pasture in the farthest corner of the kingdom. He was grazing by a fence.

"Falada!" she called. "I have found you. How are you?"

"I am well," said Falada. "I am exactly where a horse should be. But you are not where a princess should be."

The princess and her beloved Falada talked for a long time. After that, the princess insisted that she and Conrad take the geese to Falada's pasture each day. Conrad soon grew tired of trudging out to the far pasture every morning. He went to complain to the king.

"She talks to that horse all day," Conrad told him.

"And the horse talks to her?" asked the puzzled king.

"Yes," said Conrad. "He tells her how brokenhearted the queen would be to see her daughter tending geese."

The curious king visited the pasture himself. He saw that Conrad was right. The goose girl was the true princess!

That night, the king asked the lady-in-waiting a question. "If someone has deceived me by pretending she is a princess," he said, "should she be made to tend geese?"

The maid smiled, thinking he described the princess. "No, your majesty," she answered. "Such a girl belongs in the stable, cleaning up after the horses."

The king nodded. "That is just what you shall do."

When the king returned the royal ring to the princess, he humbly apologized. "I should have recognized a true princess by her goodness and grace, not by her fine clothes and jewels," he told her.

The princess forgave the king. She and the prince were soon married, and everyone lived happily ever after—except for the poor stable girl.

The Flying Prince

Adapted by Brian Conway
Illustrated by Kathi Ember

One day while Prince Rashar was exploring a new part of the jungle, a large parrot landed near him.

"I am the king of the parrots," it said proudly. "Hunters are not welcome in our kingdom."

"I will not harm you," promised Prince Rashar. "But tell me, how is it you can talk?"

"Princess Saledra gave me the power so I can protect my subjects," he answered. "She is the kindest and loveliest princess in the world!"

"Then I would like to know her," said the prince.

"It is impossible," answered the parrot. "She lives far away in the city where night becomes day."

Prince Rashar decided that he must meet this Princess Saledra. So he set off to travel to her land.

On his way, he came upon four arguing trolls.

"Excuse me," the prince said, "what is the trouble?"

"Our master left us these four magic items," the trolls answered. "But we cannot divide them fairly."

The magic items were a flying carpet, a cloth bag that produced anything wished for by its holder, a bowl that filled with water upon command, and a tool that could defeat and tie up any enemy.

"I can help you," said the clever prince. "I will shoot an arrow into the jungle. Whoever returns with the arrow shall keep all of the items."

The trolls agreed that the prince's plan was fair.

Prince Rashar shot his arrow. When the trolls began their search, the prince took the magic items for himself.

Prince Rashar sat upon the magic carpet. "Take me to the city where night becomes day," he said.

The magic carpet lifted the prince high above the jungle, and they sailed through the air. After a time, it landed near the gates of a city. Prince Rashar stopped an old woman to ask about Princess Saledra.

"Nobody sees the princess until nightfall," the woman said. "You must go to the palace and wait."

The prince hurried to the palace. When the sun set, the city was dark for a moment. Then suddenly, Princess Saledra appeared on the palace roof. Prince Rashar drew a sharp breath.

Her beauty shone more brightly than the moon. In an instant, her radiance turned night into day. The entire city was lit by the princess's glow.

Prince Rashar was in love.

Prince Rashar took his magic bag and said, "Give me a shawl that matches the princess's gown."
He reached in and pulled out a flowing silk shawl.

"Carpet," he said, "take me to Princess Saledra's chamber." The flying carpet set him down gently on the palace roof. The prince crept through the window and into the princess's room.

Princess Saledra slept soundly in her bed. The prince set the shawl beside her, and stopped to gaze upon her beautiful face. Then he left quietly.

The next morning, the princess awoke to find the beautiful shawl. Who had been able to match the magical silk of her dress? Princess Saledra was curious about who her secret admirer could be.

"To make such a perfect shawl," she thought, "he must have magic as strong as my own."

The next evening, Prince Rashar flew again to the princess's window. This time he knocked softly.

When Princess Saledra saw him standing on the flying carpet, she knew it was her mysterious admirer.

"Dear Princess," said the prince, bowing, "I am Prince Rashar. I have traveled far to meet you. Unlike your own great magic, mine comes from these four objects. I present them to you as tokens of my love."

The princess saw that the prince spoke from his heart. Her own heart softened when she considered the sacrifice of his gifts. The princess smiled at the prince, the brightest smile ever seen. The prince smiled back, reflecting her radiance.

Princess Saledra stepped gracefully onto the magic carpet. Then the two sailed off together, through the night that shone like day.

Thumbelina

Adapted by Lynne Roberts
Illustrated by Jane Maday

Once there was a woman who lived alone in a tiny cottage. She loved her beautiful garden and the birds that sang there. But she longed for a child to share her joy.

One day, an old peddler woman came to her gate.

"I believe I have something that can help you," the peddler told her kindly. She pulled a small bundle from one of her pockets. "Take these seeds and plant them in your garden. Within a month, you will find your heart's desire. I wish you luck, my dear."

The woman thanked the peddler and planted the seeds. As soon as she watered them, a beautiful tulip grew from the earth.

"What a lovely flower," said the woman. She bent down to kiss its delicate petals. When she did, the petals opened! Sitting in the center of the flower was the most beautiful child she had ever seen.

"Dear child," she said, "you are no bigger than my thumb. I will call you Thumbelina."

The woman cared for Thumbelina like her own daughter. They spent their days in the garden, and the woman was perfectly contented at last.

One day, the woman stepped inside the cottage for a moment while Thumbelina played merrily in the garden. The tiny girl's sweet singing attracted the attention of an ugly toad who was hopping by.

"She is a pretty little thing," he thought to himself. "I would like to make her my wife."

The toad snatched Thumbelina from the garden and brought her to his lily pad in a distant pond.

"Wait here while I make our wedding preparations," he told her.

Thumbelina strained to glimpse the edge of the pond. But the water stretched as far as she could see. She knelt on the lily pad and began to cry.

Her tears made ripples in the pond and brought some curious fish to the surface. They took pity on the girl and nibbled through the lily pad's stem. They floated the lily pad down the stream. As she alighted on the shore, Thumbelina thanked the fish for their help.

She walked as far as her legs could carry her, but she did not know where to find her mother's garden. As night fell, she wove a tiny hammock from blades of grass.

Thumbelina searched the woods for many weeks, looking for her mother. Then the leaves changed colors and the nights grew colder as winter approached.

One day, Thumbelina wandered farther than ever before. As night began to fall, she found herself a great distance from her shelter. A wolf howled in the distance, and Thumbelina began to run. In her haste, she tripped over a tree root and fell.

Suddenly, she saw a small door in the bottom of the tree trunk!

Thumbelina knocked shyly. The door opened a crack, and a little field mouse peered out. When the mouse saw the lovely girl on her doorstep, she invited her in to warm herself by the fire. After hearing of Thumbelina's plight, the kind mouse invited her to stay through the winter.

Thumbelina helped the field mouse gather food and supplies for the cold months ahead, and then the two friends settled down together in the burrow.

One day, a strange sound brought the field mouse and Thumbelina to the window. There they saw a sparrow with an injured wing. He had been traveling south for the winter, but now he could no longer fly. The sparrow knew he could not survive the cold winter outside.

The hospitable field mouse welcomed the sparrow into her home. Thumbelina helped him into the burrow and tried to make him comfortable.

The sparrow was surprised to see such a tiny person living with the field mouse.

"Are you a fairy princess?" he asked Thumbelina.

"What is a fairy?" she asked.

"Someday, when my wing is better, I will show you," answered the sparrow.

Thumbelina asked if he was one of the lovely birds that had taught her to sing in her mother's garden. He was not, but his cousin had told him stories of singing with a tiny girl.

Thumbelina was overjoyed. "Yes! It was I who sang with your cousin! What a glorious voice he has."

Thumbelina began to sing for the sparrow and the little field mouse. They were delighted by her sweet voice and insisted that she sing for them every day.

The winter passed quite quickly in the snug little burrow. The sparrow's wing soon healed, and the friends entertained themselves with stories and songs. They even built a tiny stage for themselves from a human-sized thimble.

Although she was happy, all winter long Thumbelina continued to dream of her mother and their garden. She longed to return to her home.

When spring arrived, the sparrow offered to carry Thumbelina to her mother's cottage. They parted sadly from their friend the field mouse. Then they flew off into the fresh spring air.

"I have a surprise for you, Thumbelina," the sparrow told her as he landed on a flower. "I have brought you to the land where the fairies live, as I promised."

Just then, a white flower opened to reveal a perfect little boy. He was the same size as Thumbelina! On his back was a pair of wings, and he also wore a tiny golden crown. He was the prince of the fairies!

The prince asked Thumbelina to be his bride. He placed a golden crown on her head. Then, two smaller fairies fastened a pair of delicate wings onto her back.

Thumbelina curtsied in pleasure, happy to have found creatures like her.

"I will marry you, Prince," she answered happily. "But you and the fairies must come live with me in my mother's garden. I will never be happy anywhere else."

The sparrow guided Thumbelina and the other fairies back to her mother's home. When they arrived, the woman was overjoyed to see her dear daughter again! She was also delighted by the fairies.

Every summer the sparrow visited the garden, where they all lived happily ever after.

The Little Mermaid

Adapted by Natasha Reed
Illustrated by John Martinez

Deep in the ocean, a sea king lived in a castle made of coral. His kingdom was filled with colorful plants that swayed gracefully in the currents. Fish of all shapes and sizes glided between their branches, as birds do on land.

The sea king had six daughters. The youngest was the loveliest of all. She was quiet and thoughtful, and she had the most beautiful singing voice of all the mermaids in the kingdom.

Nothing gave the youngest princess more pleasure than to hear about the world above the sea. It seemed wonderful to her that the flowers on land had fragrance and that the fish—which were called birds there—could sing.

On her fifteenth birthday, each princess was allowed to visit the water's surface for the first time. Year after year, the little mermaid watched her older sisters take their turns. They were delighted with what they saw. But soon, since they could go up whenever they pleased, the older girls became indifferent.

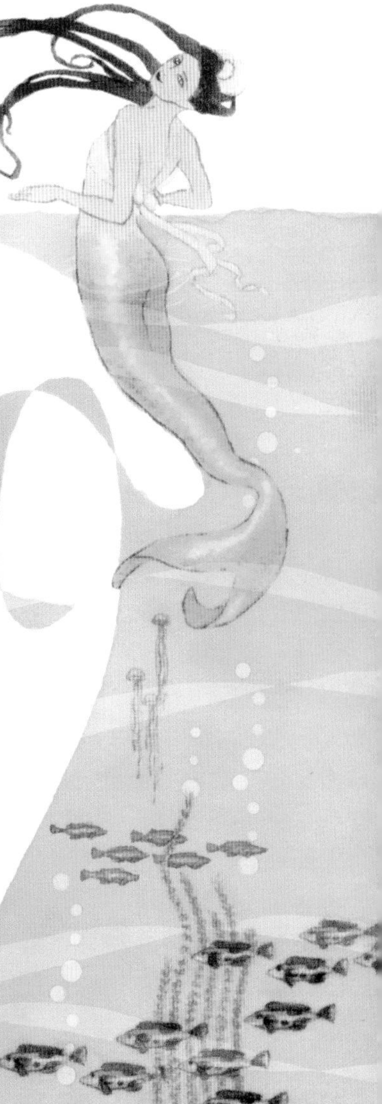

Finally, it was the little mermaid's turn. She waved good-bye to her sisters and rose swiftly to the surface.

As she broke through the water, the little mermaid saw a large ship. Strange music spilled from the deck and hundreds of colored lanterns were lit in celebration. She swam closer and saw a handsome young prince. She watched him for a long time and realized it was his birthday, too.

The wind began to blow harder, and the sky grew very dark. Pounding waves battered the prince's ship, and she could hear it creak and groan.

Suddenly, in a flash of lightning, she saw the handsome prince fall into the sea and begin to sink.

At first the little mermaid was happy that the handsome prince would come to her father's kingdom. But then she remembered that the human prince could not survive beneath the sea.

She dove under the waves and used all of her strength to pull the prince's head above the water. Then she brought him safely to shore.

Tenderly, the little mermaid brushed the hair from the prince's face and bent her head to kiss his forehead. When she heard excited shouts from the other end of the beach, she knew that she must leave him.

She took one last look at the prince, then quickly slipped beneath the surface of the water.

For many days, the little mermaid could think of nothing but the handsome prince. When she told her sisters, they wept with her.

"Perhaps the sea witch will agree to help you," they said.

The brave little mermaid went to the sea witch at once. When she arrived, the witch knew why she had come.

"Princess, I can give you human legs so you can walk and dance on land," she said. "But in return, you must give me your lovely voice."

The little mermaid agreed to her terms.

The witch prepared the magic potion and sealed it tightly in a bottle. Then she captured the little mermaid's voice, so the girl could neither speak nor sing.

The little mermaid swam to the surface and drank the potion without hesitation. She felt quite strange, and her tail began to ache. Then, before her eyes, her tail transformed into two beautiful human legs!

The prince was on his morning walk when he discovered the beautiful, silent girl on the beach. Not knowing how else to help her, he brought her with him to the palace.

The little mermaid was given gowns of fine silk and muslin to wear. She was the most beautiful creature in the palace. But she could not communicate with her voice.

Instead, the girl used her graceful movements and expressive eyes to speak to those around her. She danced and glided on her new legs as though she were swimming on land.

Everyone in the palace was enchanted by the little mermaid, especially the prince. He felt as if he had met her before.

Everywhere the prince went, the little mermaid was by his side. They rode together on horseback through the sweet-scented woods. Green boughs touched their shoulders, and little birds sang among the fresh leaves.

She climbed with the prince to the tops of tall mountains. They wound their way higher and higher until they could see soft clouds far below them.

As the days passed, the little mermaid loved the prince more dearly. And he also grew very fond of her.

At night, when the royal household was asleep, the little mermaid would follow the broad marble steps from the palace down to the water's edge. There she would sit in the moonlight and bathe her weary feet in the cool seawater. Her thoughts would turn to her beloved family, deep in the water below.

One night, her sisters rose to the surface, singing sorrowfully as they floated on the water. She beckoned to them, and they recognized her and swam closer. They told the little mermaid how much they missed her. They pleaded with her to return with them to their land beneath the sea.

The little mermaid smiled at them. She wanted to tell them how happy she was! She could only gesture with her eyes and the graceful movements of her hands and arms. She tried to explain how wonderful it was to be with the prince.

Her sisters were comforted to see that the little mermaid was happy. After that, her sisters came to the palace every night to visit her.

Once, she even saw her father in the distance. He had not been to the surface in many years and so did not venture so near the land as her sisters.

One day, the prince and the little mermaid returned from a walk in the gardens to find the king and queen waiting to speak with the prince. They had made the acquaintance of a neighboring king, and they believed his daughter, the princess, would make a suitable bride for him.

The little mermaid felt a sudden chill. After all she had sacrificed to be with the prince, would he choose to marry another?

At the thought, her expressive eyes became brilliant with tears. Yet she smiled at the prince.

The prince reached for the little mermaid's hand. When she turned to him, she saw a look of love.

Could her dream be coming true?

"Mother and Father," said the prince, "my true love is here. I desire no other." The prince sank to one knee and looked into the little mermaid's eyes. She bent her head to kiss the prince's cheek.

Suddenly, the little mermaid's voice returned to her. Their love had broken the sea witch's spell!

Soon after, the prince and the little mermaid were married. As they set sail on their wedding voyage, the king and queen waved from the shore. The little mermaid's sisters and father followed the ship out to sea.

The little mermaid and the handsome prince lived happily ever after.

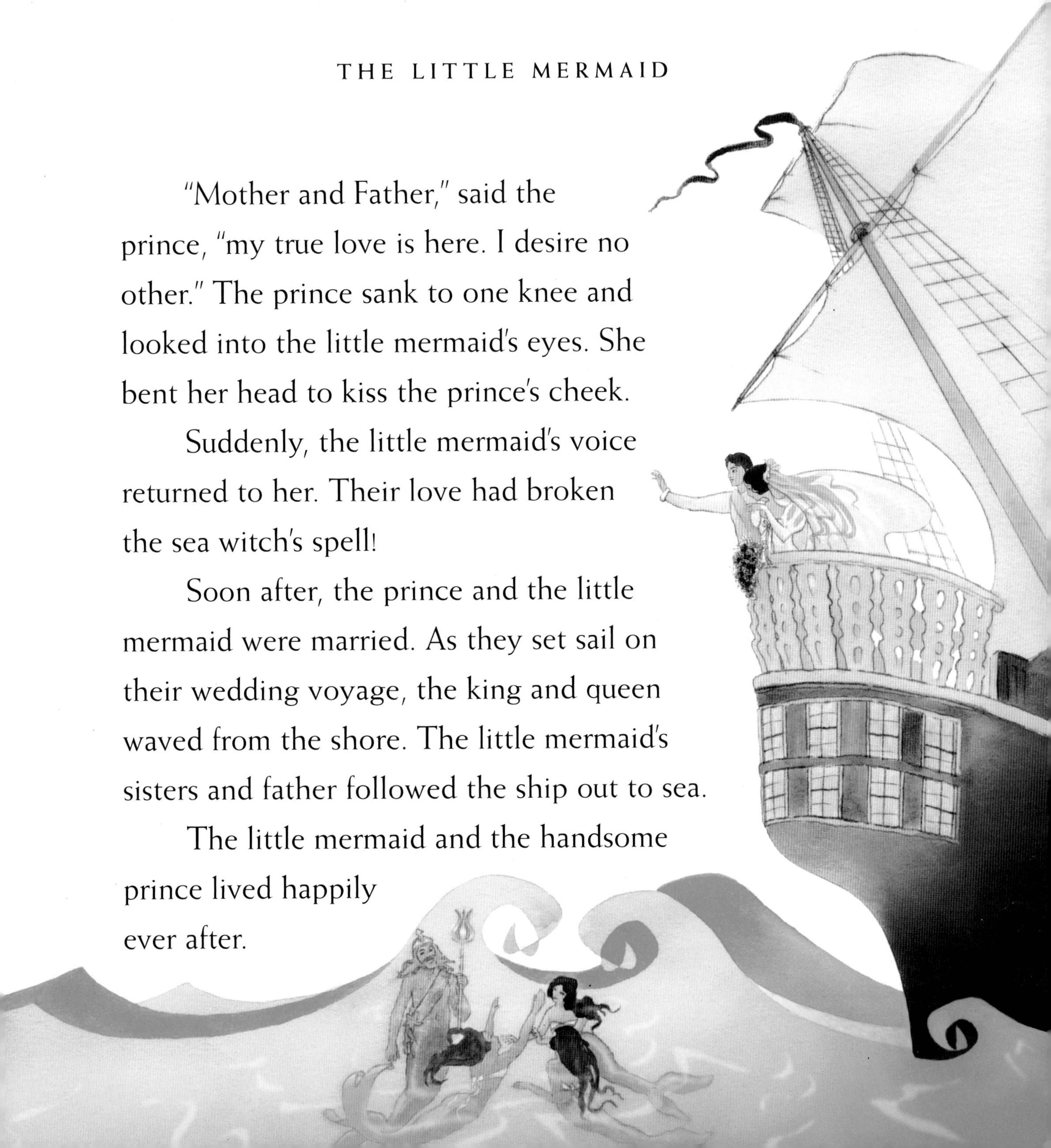

The End